Sweetest of Fires

Hayley Briana

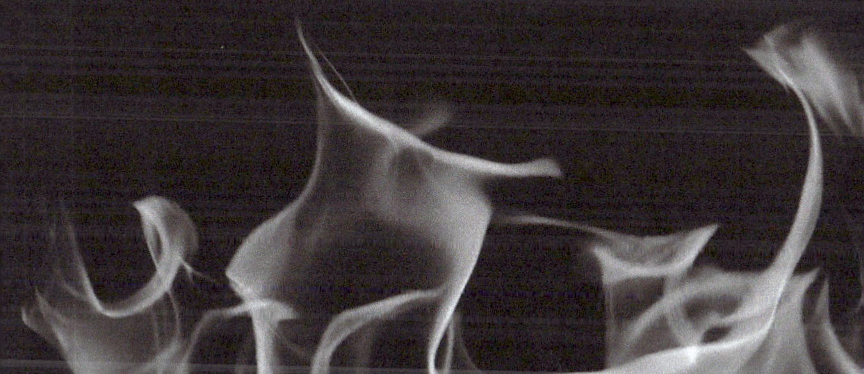

Wouldn't we all like someone who would burn this world for us?

NOTE TO THE READER

This work is a prequel for The Hellfire Novellas, "Angel of Blood" and "Angel in Chains." This prequel can be read either before or after the novellas. It follows the story of how Hellfire came to be, as well as how Cherry and Dimitri found each other.

This book contains explicit content and dark themes that may be traumatic and offensive to some readers. It is intended only for those 18 years or older.

For a full list of triggers, please visit the author's website HayleyBrianaWrites.com

*****This may be my darkest book as of its publication. Please take your own mental health into consideration and read the triggers before reading this book.*****

Scan with your phone camera to see a full list of triggers

Playlist

"Serotonin - Acoustic" - JESSIA

"Half Life" - Livingston

"She's an Actor" - Austin Giorgio

"Unlovable" - DIAMANTE

"Ocean Eyes" - Billie Eilish

"We Don't Have To Dance" - Andy Black

"Hold Me" - SkyDxddy

"Make It Home" - DEZI

"I Wouldn't Love Me" - Sam Short

"Love Me Harder" - Steven Rodriguez

Prologue

It was so dark in my room as I hid under the covers.

Daddy had his business people over tonight, and I didn't want any of them to know I was in here.

Those men were so mean. Touching places they had no business. But daddy never believed me. He thought mommy was enough for them.

I could hear the noises coming from downstairs. I didn't like the sounds, but the wall and covers weren't enough to drown them out.

The door opened, and I froze, not even willing to breathe as I clenched the covers tighter around me.

I wanted to scream for help, but no one would ever come help.

Chapter One

Cherry

"Miss Vahn, we regret to inform you that you will not be allowed to continue this semester at the University. We expect you to pack your things and leave campus within the next 48 hours. If you fail to do so, you will be escorted from campus and charged with trespassing. Is that understood?" The head of the school board, Francis McCormick, said in his pompous voice. His balding head glaring in the overhead lights.

"I understand." I clenched my hands in my lap, wrinkling the pencil skirt in my fingers.

Looking over at the man who got me into this mess, I saw that he wasn't even looking in my direction. Not once during this hearing had he stood up to defend me. His eyes never looked in my direction.

According to his statement, I had seduced him. When in all reality he'd been the one to first speak to me in that damned bar a month before the start of my first semester. I'd made it clear then that I was an eighteen-year-old who was starting the psych program at the university. Never mentioning during those first few weeks that he was a professor at the school. No, that had only happened after I'd walked into my intro to psychology class and found him at the front writing his name on the board.

He'd avoided me like the plague since that other student walked in on us in his office last week. My dress bunched around my waist as he thrust into me.

It hadn't been my fault he'd forgotten to lock the door, yet I was the one being punished. Professor Jackson Stewart would be on probation, but not removed from the school. I, however, was forced to leave without finishing my last semester for my degree in psychology. Ending any progress I'd made towards my new life or starting my Master's degree. The school had already rejected me from the program.

In all honesty, I probably should have known better. I should have called off what we had when I found out he was a psychology professor at the start of my first year. I knew what would happen if I got involved with a teacher. Yet Jackson had insisted he loved me. That we could be careful and keep our relationship a secret. At least until I graduated and we could get married. No one would bat an eye at the wife of a professor, right?

We had been so careful. Never going out in public together. No one ever saw me enter his house. Keeping my dorm room so that I always had an alibi. Going to parties only to sneak out to park down the road from his house for the night. Making sure not to get caught. But one slip up on his part was all it took to have my world crashing down around me.

I could still see the horror on his face when that girl had walked in. Catching us in a position, there was no way to explain away. She'd done the right thing by reporting it, and I didn't blame her. I could only blame myself for everything that was happening. I'd let my love struck heart get in the way of what I knew was wrong.

I left the meeting with the school board as quickly as possible. Jackson didn't deserve my tears. He'd made me believe he loved me these past 4 years, but the moment things got hard he did what he did best. Shutting down and avoiding me as if I were the problem. This wouldn't be like every other obstacle we'd faced. There would be no hate filled makeup sex. No, *I'm sorry* and no fixing what had obviously been broken for a long time. Maybe from the very beginning.

He was no better than any other man. The only men worth my time were my brother and childhood friends. They didn't even know about what had been going on.

I'd made sure to keep my relationship with Jackson a secret. Even from my twin brother and friends. I'd planned on telling them after I graduated and there was no issue with us being together. I would have graduated and it wouldn't be seen as a student and teacher affair. At least that's what Jackson had me believe.

Zack would be pissed on my behalf, and Damon would want to kill Jackson, which was a real possibility with him.

I'd have to call them eventually, but today I would pack my things into my car and get all the tears out of my system. I could call Zack on the way back to that hellhole of a city. He'd at least let me stay at his place until I figured things out for myself.

I didn't let my tears fall until I was safe in my dorm room. My roommate, thankfully, was in classes for the next few hours.

Sliding down the door, I curled in on myself and cried. Cried for the future I'd worked so hard for being ripped away from me and for the love I thought I'd found with Jackson.

For a moment, I let myself break. Let myself be that broken girl I'd always known I was.

I'd pick up the pieces later.

Chapter Two

Cherry

My bags dropped onto the hardwood floors behind me, causing me to jump as I turned to look at my twin brother.

"Thank you again, Zack. I promise I'll be out of your hair as soon as I can. Maybe a week or two tops."

His hand slid through his blonde hair, and he rolled his green eyes at my comment. We looked so much alike. The same hair and eyes that we got from our druggy whore of a mother. I wasn't sure which would have been worse. Being more like our mother or our heartless father.

"Shut up. I have an extra room and there's no rush to leave. Stay as long as you want and you know that Damon is going to give you a job at Hellfire." Zack closed and locked the door before flopping onto the large sectional sofa.

He grabbed the bowl of peanuts off the coffee table. It had been his way of coping after getting off all the pills and drugs. I was just glad he could get better, unlike our mother.

Our mother had died of an overdose when we were young, not even teenagers. It left us completely at our father's mercy. We'd been fortunate to know Damon. He had been like the protective fun uncle or older brother when we were younger. He and his brother, Dimitri, took us in whenever we needed it until we were old enough to go out into the world on our own. Until we received our trust funds.

At eighteen, we'd both packed our bags and left. Zack off to get himself clean, while I took my part of our trust fund and hightailed it out of the place we'd called home.

I wanted an escape. To build my life away from the traumas of my past. To go somewhere that no one knew who I was or the dirty dealings the Vahn family were known for.

I shook my head at him, taking a seat next to him and turning on the TV.

"Let me guess? Marvel marathon?" Zack asked, offering me the bowl of peanuts.

Smiling, I took a peanut and turned on *The Avengers*. "More like Loki. One movie and then I'll put my things away in the room."

Again, I received an eye roll, but Zack never complained about my creature comforts. Whoever said that Tom Hiddleston playing Loki wasn't hot was completely wrong.

We settled on the couch and watched the movie. The single movie turned into an actual marathon until we were ordering dinner to be delivered.

It was nice to have just one day of peace before I have to deal with the shit show my life had become.

Chapter Three

Cherry

Beethoven's 5th Symphony played for the third time on my phone. A clear sign that father dearest was trying to reach me. I hadn't told him about school and had no interest in talking with him, now or ever.

For the past four years, I'd taken nothing from him save for the trust fund I was entitled to on my eighteenth birthday. That money had paid for school and my simple living. I still had some, but not enough to keep me out of work now that I was no longer focusing on my degree.

I hadn't even bothered to speak to him since I left. There was nothing to say between us anymore, not after everything he'd put me through growing up.

I let the phone go to voicemail again, sighing when he actually did leave a message this time. I sat down on my bed in Zack's guest room and hit the play button. Already preparing for the worst

"Cherry, I know you're home and I know what you did at that school. How dare you disgrace our family name? Just like your mother and brother…" I deleted the message before it was finished. I didn't need or want to hear any of it. Me getting involved with a professor was nothing compared to the dirty business dealings he was involved with.

Laying back on the bed, I stared up at the ceiling fan as its blades turned. Tonight was the grand opening of Damon's club and my first night of work. He'd offered me a job as a server and refused to take no for an answer. Zack had been put in charge of the bar and was currently there, helping to get everything set up for the big night.

"Just a nap." I whispered to myself, closing my eyes to rest.

I was running in the wooded area surrounding the house, looking for a place to hide, while I could hear Damon and Zack shouting. I clutched the paintball gun in my hand, knowing they'd be coming to find me.

Running into a clearing, I stopped short, nearly face planting into the dirt, seeing Demitri sitting against a tree with a book in his hand. He might have been only a year older than Damon, but he seemed so much older than me now. A full sixteen years older than my seventeen.

He'd never wanted to get involved in anything we did. Forcing Damon to take on the fun role of keeping a couple of teenagers entertained. I'd assumed he'd be working today, like every other day, not out here of all places reading.

I frowned, used to only seeing him in passing since he became the VP of his father's company. Always dressed in expensive suits and working on his phone when he wasn't in the office. The rare moments for his reading time decreased significantly. He'd used to read to me sometimes when he'd been younger and we'd first come to stay with the Ashford's. A part of me missing that little piece of him I got before he became a real grown up.

He looked up at me briefly before going back to his book.

"What are you reading?" I asked before I could think better of it. A heated blush creeping across my face.

I hadn't meant to ask or bother him, but I was curious. I'd always found Dimitri interesting, and if I were being honest, had a crush on him from the moment I was old enough to have any interest in boys. I was much too young for him, but knowing that didn't seem to stop the feelings.

"The Divine Comedy." His answer was clipped. If he ever deemed to respond to anyone, his answers were short, usually with a glare in the speaker's direction. The only person who ever saw a caring side of him being his brother behind closed doors.

Where Damon was brutish and violent, Dimitri had a savage calm about him. He was scary, and you knew not to fuck with him just based on a glance in his direction.

Before I could say anything else, I was hit with a paintball. I squealed, turning to run from Zack and Damon who were right behind me. Ducking behind a large tree, I fired back, missing every time as they closed in on me.

"Alright, alright! I give up!" I couldn't stop laughing as my heart raced. The interaction with Dimitri was forgotten for now.

Chapter Four

Cherry

Music blared through the room from tonight's DJ, as I moved from table to table, taking orders and cleaning up what I could.

It had been a really long time since I'd worked, having only worked as a spoiled little rich kid at sixteen, but it was easy to get into the swing of things. It also helped to keep my mind busy as I served drinks and helped around the bar. I didn't have the time to breathe, let alone think about the way my life had turned out.

"Hey there. What can I get for you guys?" I asked, walking up to the newest group of guys sitting in one of the sitting areas. There were mostly boys, all dressed like rich pricks, while a handful of girls danced on their laps.

They were obviously all my age, but I couldn't remember ever acting like they did. I wasn't the partying type, only going to parties in college long enough to be seen then sneak out, and I didn't like to throw my family's wealth or name around.

One guy, who looked like a basic frat boy, smiled a crooked smile and wrapped a hand around my waist. Effectively ignoring the girl next to him as he pulled me into his lap. Hand slipping down to grab my ass.

"How about you come home with me?" He smiled, oozing confidence that made me almost grimace.

Boys my age were pretty clueless about what girls actually liked and didn't give a shit about making their partner happy in bed. A one time fling right before the end of high school made that perfectly clear. Then again, after all the shit I'd been through as a kid made it hard to be with anyone. My body count being only that one time in high school and Jackson. Maybe that was why I only seemed to like older men, too.

I plastered on my sweetest fake smile and pushed myself off him. "Not tonight. What drinks would you like?"

His eye twitched in annoyance at the obvious rejection as the other guys at the table chuckled and listed off the drinks they wanted.

I rushed to the bar, grabbing everything I needed and putting it on a serving tray.

"Cherry, you good?" Zack asked, eyes traveling from me to the table of guys.

I smiled at him, "Of course. I'm just going to drop these off and keep doing my rounds."

I knew he was worried about me, but I was okay. It wasn't the first time I'd been grabbed without my permission. I doubted it would be the last either. When you were a woman in this world, you found that most men wanted to take from you without permission.

Picking up my tray, I dropped off their drinks with a smile, keeping my distance from the handsy guy before focusing on my other tables.

I wouldn't let some drunk idiots ruin my first night at work. This was the start of a new chapter for me and I wouldn't let anyone mess this up for me.

I was exhausted as I closed the door to my room. Sliding down the wood to sit on the floor and just sitting there in the dark. It would take some time to get used to being on the move all night.

Pulling my phone from my small bag, I found an array of messages and missed calls. Signing as Jackson's face popped up on every single notification. He'd been calling and texting all night and I'd eventually just thrown my phone into a cabinet under the bar. It had been a week and now he was deciding to call me.

I shouldn't have opened anything. Just deleted the messages and blocked his number. But my heart ached at my lost love, or what I'd thought was love.

I didn't bother replying, just blocked his number and turned off the phone. I knew I shouldn't have looked at the damn things.

Tossing the phone onto the carpeted floor, not caring if I ever looked at it again. There was no energy left in me to deal with any of it, especially tonight.

I refused to let myself break again. I'd cried the day it all happened and wouldn't cry over him anymore. Jackson wasn't worth another second of my time.

It was time to get some rest.

Chapter Five

Cherry

Over the next few weeks, I found myself getting into the swing of things. I spent most days resting and worked night shifts at Hellfire. The work kept me busy and most of the time it was easy to ignore the idiot guys who showed up from time to time. The club was always packed and had become one of the hottest places to be in the city..

Zack had to let the bouncer, Ray, know what had been going on with the handsy guys and he made sure to kick anyone out who bothered me or got too close.

It had been sweet of Damon to offer me the full-time job, which included benefits, allowing me to save up money. I was positive that soon I'd have the chance to move out to my own place.

While I loved my brother, he was a bit of a man whore. He always brought home girls from the club and I wasn't interested in hearing the noises from down the hall. The boy seriously needed to soundproof his room or something.

And I needed my space. Somewhere that I could just be me without anyone else around. I'd never had that and quiet seemed like a good idea.

I'd already applied to rent a few places I was sure I could afford on my own. All within a short distance from the club so that I could walk to work.

It was time I learned to stand on my own two feet and not rely on the other people in my life for everything. I'd never ask another man to take care of me. I was sure at this point that I was the issue or just had horrible taste in men.

With my mind made up, I dressed for work in a vintage tee, black jean shorts that were ripped in places, and a pair of converse. Throwing my shoulder length hair back in a bun and applying light makeup, I left out the bedroom door.

Zack was standing in the kitchen with his latest conquest, and I made sure not to look in their direction as I left. From the sound, they were trying to suck each other's faces off.

Chapter Six

Dimitri

My brother's club had been open for two weeks now and of course father wished to have his meetings there this evening. He couldn't allow Damon to have anything of his own, so moving his less unsavory business deals to Hellfire was a public *fuck you* to his youngest son.

I was finishing up some last-minute paperwork before leaving the office to meet them there. If things went as usual, it would be a shit show. I could imagine my brother flipping tables and threatening to murder them and their families.

"Mr. Ashford, your car is here." Susie, my newest assistant, said from the doorway.

I didn't bother looking in her direction as I signed the last contract of the day. The rest could wait until tomorrow. My father might be a legitimate owner in the tech and security sector, but he made the most through his dealings on nights like this one.

If it weren't for me, this company would be in hot water. While my father focused on the dark underground business, I was the face of the legitimate business. I was the VP and lifeblood of this company, and I would never allow him to destroy the cleanest money our family had access to.

He'd raised me to be the business executive, to take over when he stepped down. While he had raised Damon to be the hammer he wielded against those who sought to dethrone the Ashford legacy.

Damon had decided years ago that he would no longer support our father. Going out on his own and building a life for himself that the old man couldn't touch. He'd used the money he'd earned through his less than unsavory ventures to split from the Ashford line as soon as he was able.

He'd been the smarter brother.

I pushed away from the desk, grabbing my suit jacket from the back of my chair as I walked out.

"Have a nice evening, Mr. Ashford."

I glanced over at Susie. "You as well."

The secretaries never lasted here long, especially with how my father went through them, and I didn't bother to get to know any of them. They were all the same, just looking for a way to fuck their way into someone else's fortune. When they realized I wasn't interested, they went to the big boss man himself.

Now that I thought about it, it had been years since I'd found a woman worth a second of my time. Nothing ever lasted long when they realized I didn't have time for them, preferring work to any sort of intimate relationship. Making sure my father didn't run our company to the ground, taking up all my time. Finding someone who didn't require me home at night or to be emotionally available hadn't been easy. Hence, having no love life to speak of.

I slid into the car, flipping through emails on my phone as the driver drove us to Hellfire. It would only take about twenty minutes to get there. While sitting here in the back of a car, I could get some correspondents off my to-do list.

"We are here, Mr. Ashford." The driver said as we pulled into the parking lot.

The large skull logo that read hellfire in orange and cold lighting up the front of the building. From the outside, it looked more like a giant biker bar than a lavish club. Inside, however, was the perfect mix of grunge and sophistication, the perfect mixture to describe my younger brother. Featuring slick wooden floors, neon lights, seating areas, pool tables in the back, and an upstairs lounge for Damon to watch over his passion project. It had been what made the place so popular. Drawing in crowds of the wealthy and civilians simply looking for a night out.

I didn't bother to answer the driver as I climbed out of the car, buttoning my suit jacket as I stood and looked around. There was already a long line out the front and music blasting from the open front doors.

Not bothering with the line, I walked directly up to the door where the bouncer, Ray, ushered me inside. Some in the crowd bitched that I'd been allowed to walk in. If only they knew who I really was. The thing that kept most of them from learning the darker truths of this city.

Fucking commoners didn't realize the people who ran their city, many far worse than me.

"Dimitri." I heard my name called in a deep rumble and turned to face my younger brother.

"Damon." My voice was monotone and bored as I looked around at all the patrons inside the place.

While my brother had always been the unruly of sorts, he was intelligent in his own way. He'd built this place from nothing without the aid of our father, leaving the abrasive life behind. No longer the enforcer for all the things the old man had him involved in. He'd taken a life far too young, in my opinion, and it had fucked him up. Now the blood and pain of others was a drug he craved.

I never considered us to be mobsters, but at the end of the day there had never been anything else that accurately described the life we'd been raised in. We may have wealth and look like proper gentlemen, but we were really the monsters lurking in the shadows. Enough assets that we could line the pockets of every person we needed to look the other way, or make the people who got in our way disappear.

"The old man is already upstairs if you want to head up." He blew out a ring of smoke from his cigarette as he nodded towards some stairs near the back, leading up to a windowed room that overlooked the dancefloor.

With a nod, I headed in that direction, effortlessly avoiding the grinding bodies as I made my way through the crowd. I was almost to the stairs when a smaller body crashed into me.

On instinct, I reached out, grabbing the woman around the waist before she could fall to the floor. I may have been a heartless bastard, but I wouldn't put a woman on her ass anywhere outside the bedroom.

"Shit! I'm so sor-" the words were cut short as I looked down into a familiar pair of green eyes.

"Cherry." I said, making sure she had her footing before I backed up a step. Thankfully, her tray had been empty when we had collided. I wasn't in the mood to change into new clothes so late.

"Dimitri," she sounded breathless as she looked up at me. I was a good foot taller than her 5'2" frame.

I wasn't aware she'd even come back. It had been nearly four years since she'd been in town. Running off as soon as she was of age to go somewhere to get her degree. Not that I blamed her for leaving. She'd had a rough childhood.

She had changed so much, her golden blonde hair cut just past her shoulders, styled to look wavy, with light makeup to show off her natural beauty. She was no longer the little girl who'd frequented our home. It was obvious as her breasts spilled from the cut in her t-shirt.

My cock jerked to attention as my eyes roamed over her, watching a light blush grace her freckled cheeks. No, she was not the little girl or teenager who had lived in my home. She was the figment of my deepest desires and darkest cravings. When she'd begun to grow into a woman, it had been hard to control the darker thoughts. Imagining what her tight cunt would have felt like wrapped around my cock. The fantasies of her consumed my mind, even back then when she was far too young, until my hand wrapped around my length, searching for any sort of release. I'd always hated myself afterwards. Knowing she was too young and had already been used too much by the men her father allowed into his home.

"Be more careful, Cherry." I said, walking past her and up the stairs. I could feel her eyes on my back until I entered the room upstairs.

Chapter Seven

Cherry

Shit.

I'd just run into Dimitri and I couldn't convince my heart to stop racing as I watched him walk upstairs..

Shaking my head, I rushed back to the bar to grab my orders. Zack's eyes were on me the entire time as I grabbed bottles and glasses to fill orders.

"How was your talk with Dimitri?" Zack asked. I could hear the smirk in his voice as I finished mixing the last drink.

"Shut up." I huffed out, turning to face him.

Sure enough, his smile was wide as he watched me. My face grew hotter, and I turned my head, hoping that my hair was hiding the blush covering my cheeks.. I'd always had a crush on Dimitri and Zack had used every opportunity to make fun of me for it. He didn't seem to mind the thought of me and Dimitri. Nothing had ever happened between us, so I doubted anything ever would.

"You still don't have a crush do you, sis? I bet getting under him would definitely help you get over that professor of yours."

I groaned in irritation and embarrassment, grabbing my tray and getting back to work.

Thankfully, Dimitri had stayed upstairs the entire night, so there was no reliving my embarrassment. We were just closing up and once everything was finished, I could go back to Zack's and hopefully get some sleep for once.

I hadn't been sleeping well since I'd been back. All the memories I'd worked so hard to forget came back the longer I was here. Nightmares waking me from sleep as I cried into my pillow, hoping to not wake my brother and whatever date he'd brought home for the night.

My father had finally stopped calling and leaving messages. Things were overall quiet save for my embarrassing run in with my childhood crush tonight, anyway.

"Hey Cherry! Check the back to make sure no one else is here before I lock up." Damon yelled out as he finished cleaning up the bar with Zack.

I smiled with a nod in his direction before heading to the back. It was a long, dark hallway where you could find the offices, supply room, bathrooms, and the door that led to the basement. I was fully aware of what was down those stairs and had no interest in ever seeing it. Damon had a weird love for basements and I didn't want to accidentally walk in on his newest toy.

With a shake of my head to clear the disturbing thought, I stuck my head into the women's bathroom first just to make sure no one had been left inside.

"If anyone is in here we are closed." I said, my voice echoing off the bathroom walls.

Satisfied it was empty I moved to close the door when hands grabbed me, pushing me forward into the wall between the two bathroom doors.

"Well, aren't you a pretty thing?" Beer breath fanned over my neck and face as the man pushed me against the wall.

"Get the hell off me!" I yelled, bracing my hands on the wall for leverage. I threw my head back., hearing a sickening crunch as the back of my head made contact with the guy's face. Causing my vision to swim at the impact. Feelings as if my brain were shaking in my head.

"You bitch." The guy went to grab me again, pressing me back against the wall. I could feel his blood soaking into the back of my shirt from his broken nose. His hands pulled at my shorts, trying to push them down as he crushed my hands between my body and the wall. I'd hoped the broken nose would have given me a chance to slip away, but the alcohol had to be at play, numbing his pain.

Panic took over as I struggled to get away. My voice caught in my throat as this drunk idiot tried to force himself on me. A growl of frustration sounded as he struggled to force my shorts down my legs.

Everything happened so fast. One minute I was pressed against the wall and the next the weight on my back was gone. The sound of skin making an impact with

skin and bones crunching the only sound as I turned to
see what happened.

Dimitri was on top of the guy, rearranging his face
with his fist. My back hit the wall, and I slid down it. Just
staring wide eyed at the bloody mess before me.

Dimitri stood from the heap of a man on the
floor, taking out a handkerchief from his suit pocket and
wiped the blood from his fist. His knuckles stained red and
his jaw set in a firm line as he looked over at the man he'd
just knocked out.

He bent down in front of me, taking my face in
his hands so that I was forced to look at him. His thumb
wiping tears from my cheeks.

"It's alright, princess." His deep voice was almost a
whisper as he slid his hand into my hair. The use of the old
nickname he'd given me as a kid sending an unexpecting
warmth to my chest.

I couldn't bring myself to say anything as the
shock set in. My face must have shown whatever I was
feeling, because he lifted me into his arms and I buried my
face in his neck. His spicy amber and oak scent washed

over me, calming my fraying nerves as I just let him hold me.

Why did this keep happening to me?

Chapter Eight

Dimitri

Anger still radiated from my every pore as I carried Cherry out to the bar. Zack and Damon rushed over as they saw me carrying Cherry back out of the hall.

Damon didn't have to ask what had happened, walking back through the hallway. My brother was homicidal on a good day, and I couldn't find the heart to care what would happen to the fucker who was bleeding back there. Maybe it had been a good thing that I'd rearranged his fucking face

"What the hell happened?" Zack asked, slipping his hand into Cherry's hair to look her over.

She didn't move from my arms, just let him look her over after I sat her on a stool at the bar.

"Some asshole in the hall." I said through clenched teeth.

"I'm okay." Cherry's soft voice came, but she still seemed out of it, staring into space. Looking at her brother without really seeing him. Her body shook as she gripped the bottom of her shirt and pulled it over her head.

I turned to look away quickly as she began to scrub the blood from her skin with a rag from the bar. I'd only seen a glimpse of pink lace before turning my head. Now was not the time to be examining a woman who'd just been assaulted.

"Shit Cherry, calm down. Let me see, and I'll clean it up." I heard Zack say.

"I need it off." Her usually sweet and bubbly voice sounded strained from the stress and her tears.

"I know. I've got it, I promise." Zack sounded frantic as he tried to keep her calm.

I looked over to watch him scrubbing the blood from her back. Only now noticing a large cherry blossom tree tattoo covering her back now that she'd turned to face the bar, giving Zack better access to wipe the blood off her back.

She'd managed to break the guy's nose before I'd shown up. The thought making me wish I'd done more than break his fucking face.

She just sat there in a bra and shorts as her brother helped clean her. I took off my jacket and looked over my dress shirt. It luckily hadn't gotten dirty in the chaos and I began to unbutton it. Pulling the fabric off my shoulders as Zack finished cleaning the blood from her skin. He moved around the bar to toss the rag, and I placed the shirt on Cherry's shoulders. Helping her slip her arms into the sleeves and buttoning up the front. Making sure not to stare at the thin, see-through pink lace of her bra, which left little to the imagination.

The shirt wasn't the best, but at least it was clean and would keep her covered and warm.

"Thank you." Her words were still a whisper as she looked up at me. She'd finally stopped crying. Her mascara streaked down her pretty face.

"I'll take care of her. I'm going to take her home. Go find out what Damon is doing back there." Zack said, walking around to look over at his sister again.

I nodded, placing a light kiss on Cherry's hair. Her cherry blossom scent enveloping me for a moment, before heading towards the basement. I wasn't going to let my brother have all the fun tonight.

Chapter Nine

Cherry

Damon had given me some time off from work, but I wasn't sure what to do with myself without something to keep me distracted. I

I had cleaned the entire apartment from top to bottom and was now sitting at the kitchen counter, going through a list of places I could rent. It was only me, so studios would be the most reasonable choice. I might have been born into money, but I didn't see the point of having a big place just for myself.

I was pulled from my scrolling when there was a light knock on the door. Getting up to check through the peephole, I was surprised to see Dimitri standing there, a bag in his hand, dressed in a navy Armani suit. The man knew how to wear blue, making his ocean eyes pop. He wasn't wearing a tie and had left the top buttons of his white dress shirt unbuttoned, giving him a slightly rumpled appearance.

With a deep breath to calm myself, I opened the door for him, the smell of food filling the space.

"Dimitri, what are you doing here?" I asked, glancing up at his handsome yet stern face.

Lifting the bag, he replied, "I was out to lunch and thought you might be hungry."

I moved over to let him inside as he made his way into the small kitchen, beginning to unpack the bag of food.

"Did you bring tacos?" My mouth watered at the smell as it registered what was in the bag.

"They are still your favorite, right?" He asked, glancing my way. His face never changed from that business-like look he always had.

I wished he'd smile more. I couldn't recall a single time when I'd seen him anything less than grumpy.

I smiled instead, walking over to the counter with an added skip to my step. "You know me so well!"

Tacos had always been my favorite food and the way to my heart. Even as a child, we had made sure to have tacos once a week together. Though Dimitri never really partook in our dinners. I was honestly surprised that he'd remembered it being my favorite.

Dimitri took a seat next to me at the counter on the additional barstool and slid a tray of tacos covered in all the fixings towards me. I moved my computer to the side, squeezing one of the lime slices onto the tacos.

A moan of pleasure left me at the first bite, and I squirmed in delight. It was an explosion of flavors on my tongue. I'd missed food like this since being away. I hadn't been able to find somewhere that made tacos like these. They were from the best taco truck in the city and one of the few good things in this city.

At the noise I made, Dimitri seemed to tense and looked at me from the corner of his eye. I felt my face heat as I sat down the taco and cleared my throat.

"Sorry. They are really good. Thank you for bringing me lunch." Embarrassment threatened to heat my face as I took care to act like a lady as I went back to eating.

"You're welcome." Dimitri said, turning to his own food where we continued to eat in silence. A thick silence that didn't feel horribly uncomfortable. It was a calming sort of quiet. Like we were just enjoying each other's company.

When we were done, I took to cleaning up after us and sat back down at the counter to continue looking at places to stay.

"What made you bring me lunch, anyway?" I asked as I scrolled on my laptop.

"Damon mentioned you were off work and it was on my way back to the office. Are you looking for a new place to stay?"

"Yeah. I don't want to mooch off Zack for longer than necessary." I said, clicking on one of the cheaper options for a studio apartment.

"Can't you stay in something nicer than that with the money you got from your father?" Dimitri's tone sounded surprised as he looked at the screen.

I bit my lip as I looked over the amenities the apartment complex offered. "I don't take anything from my father other than my trust fund. Most of that went to school. There's still some left, but I don't want to only rely on that for income. It's just for me anyway, so why would I need a lot of space or anything fancy?" I was word vomiting and I wasn't really reading the listing I was scrolling through either.

He didn't reply after that, seeming content to simply watch me scroll through all the options. One was close to the bar, in a decent complex that had a public gym and indoor pool. I quickly sent an email application about renting one of the available apartments before closing the laptop.

"How long do you have for lunch?" I asked, looking towards the clock. He'd already been here for nearly an hour.

"As long as I want. The perks of being the VP," Dimitri said, leaning back in his seat. He'd removed his jacket to drape over the back of the stool and rolled up his sleeves.

I couldn't help noticing the defined muscles of his arms. The veins that pressed against his skin traveled down to some of the sexiest hands I'd ever seen on a man. Long fingers I was sure knew exactly where to touch a woman.

Crap.

What was it about arms and hands on a man that were so attractive?

The knuckles of his right hand were red and beginning to scab over. Before I could think better of it I grabbed his hand, lightly running my finger over the healing skin.

"Is this from…" I couldn't bring myself to finish the question. Expected him to pull away from me, but he didn't, just nodding his head as I looked over the wounds.

"Thank you for that, too." My voice was just over a whisper as I looked up into his ocean eyes.

"That miscreant deserved it and much worse." His voice came out deep and husky as I let go of his hand.

The same hand moved to cup my face as we looked into each other's eyes. He was so close that I could feel his breath on my lips and my heart raced in my chest.

He leaned in closer and I was sure he would kiss me. Until his phone rang. He pulled back to fish the annoying thing from his jacket pocket while I tried to get my face to cool.

"I have to take this. It was nice to see you again, Cherry." He placed a light kiss on my hair before grabbing his jacket from the back of his stool and walking out the front door without turning back.

Chapter Ten

Cherry

It had been a week since Dimitri had brought me lunch. I hadn't heard from or seen him since then. I couldn't get the thought of his touch and that almost kiss from my head in the meantime.

A part of me was wondering if I'd imagined the entire thing. There was no way Dimitri had actually been about to kiss me. Not once in the time we'd known each other had he shown any sort of interest in me other than the interest of someone he took care of when they were younger.

Even getting the call that I could move into the new place hadn't gotten the image out of my head. I could still feel his hand on my skin and found myself fantasizing about what his hands would feel like on other parts of my body.

I'd felt guilty about that, especially with how my last relationship turned out. It was time I really focused on myself for a little while. Still, that fantasy of a life with Dimitri invaded my brain the moment things got a little too quiet.

"When can you go view the apartment?" Zack asked, flipping the bottle in his hand before pouring a round of shots for the group of girls crowding the bar. He was such a show off when he was trying to impress a girl at the bar. Tonight a little brunet had his attention who wore a shiny crown in her hair and a sash that said birthday girl on it in bold pink letters.

"I'm going to get the keys in the morning and sign all the paperwork." I slid a beer across the bar for a guy who'd become a regular.

Stacking a handful of drinks onto a tray, I rolled my eyes at my brother, who was now shamelessly flirting with the group of girls.

"One day you're going to find a girl who doesn't fall for your charms." I shouted over my shoulder. He waved me off without turning his attention from the giggling girls.

Looking up at the building, I clung to Damon's arm. Zack had been too preoccupied with the brunet birthday girl from last night, so Damon had decided to tag along while looking over my new apartment. Him being the protective guy he was; I knew he'd never let me rent a shitty place or have a crappy landlord.

"It seems decent enough." Damon flashed me a crooked smile as he eyed the white bricks and golden trimming of the apartment complex. With a smile of my own, I rolled my eyes and pulled him forward. Excited to get a look at the place I'd soon be calling home. Maybe I could even get a pet to keep me company.

The place looked much nicer than it had online. Appearing as if the place was going through a remodel to make it look high end in the downtown area. Signs showcasing new penthouses on the upper floors were posted outside. I just hoped that had no effect on the cost of my rent in one of the lower studio apartments.. I could afford more, but I'd much rather save where I could.

Damon led me through the revolving door up to the front security desk. A lone security guard sat behind it flipping through today's newspaper. He was an older gentleman, possibly in his fifties or sixties. Hair salt and pepper, a matching mustache, and an aura of friendliness. He gave off the sort of grandfatherly vibes you'd see in movies featuring a sweet old man.

He flashed us a smile as we approached. "How may I help you today?"

"I'm Cherry Vahn. I came to see management about renting an apartment."

"Oh yes. The new owner has been expecting you. You're welcome to take the elevator up to the top floor. That's where he is, and he can show you around from there."

With a thanks, I pulled Damon to the elevator.

"You're awfully quiet today." I said to him as we made our way up.

"Just here for moral support." He said, pulling a cigarette from his case.

"I'm not sure you can have that in here." I pointed to a no smoking sign.

A gruff laugh left him as he lit the thing anyway, smoking slowly floating to the top of the elevator. "Rules are meant to be broken."

"Boys…" I said under my breath as the doors opened on the top floor. This was where all the penthouses would be, not where I would end up with a small apartment on the lower floors. I wondered why the manager wanted me to meet him up here just to head back down.

The sounds of power tools and shouting could be heard down the hall. We followed the sound to an open door down the hall.

A gasp left me at who I found inside. Dimitri was standing just inside. Dressed in his usual business suit and speaking to another man. He was on the shorter side, sporting a round belly, balding head, and dressed in what looked to be paint covered overalls.

An array of construction workers were around the open space. Plastic covering up most of the floor as cabinets were built and walls painted.

I could barely focus on any of it though as I stood in the doorway, wide eyes on the man before me.

Damon burst into laughter, walking past me and ashing his cigarette onto the plastic covered floor as he went.

"You can't smoke that in the building. Patio is that way." Dimitri pointed over towards what I assumed was an outdoor area through a set of French doors. Already seeming bored with his younger brother's antics.

"What the hell are you doing here?" I heard myself gasp out when Dimitri's eyes fell on me in the doorway.

"We will finish our chat later, Emry." He said to the older man who nodded and went back to shouting at the workers.

I nearly stopped breathing as Dimitri walked towards me. His stride was confident, and my face flushed from embarrassment.

"Come on, Cherry." His firm hand fell to my lower back as he led me down the hall away from all the noise of the workers. The hallways were long and appeared as if the opposite side of the building was through its renovation process.

"What are you doing here?" I asked, still sounding far too breathless for my liking.

Damn it. Why did he always make me so flustered?

"I own the building." He stated matter-of-factly as he stopped at a large white door, placing a key in the door to open it. "And this is your new apartment."

He didn't give me a chance to answer as he guided me inside. The door shut behind us with a soft click, as I took in the entryway that led directly into an open spaced kitchen to the right and living area to the left. Everything was decorated in sleek light greys and blacks. Fully furnished from the looks of it as I took in the space. Neutral art hung along the walls, all new stainless steel appliances in the kitchen, and a black leather sectional couch took up most of the space in the living area.

A large flat screen was mounted on the wall above a grey stone fireplace, cycling through images of mountain ranges and forests.

"This can't be mine." I spoke, walking deeper into the living area, fingers running slowly along the couch.

"It is, and it comes fully furnished. You're welcome to change anything you like," Dimitri said from behind me.

"I can't afford a penthouse, Dimitri." I turned to face him, a bored expression playing across his features.

He tucked his hands into his pants pockets. "You have been a friend of the Ashford family for many years and we've spent the majority of your life making sure you're taken care of.. Your money is no good here. You can move in immediately. If you need anything, just inform me or Damon."

He pulled the key back from his pocket, placing it on the counter that separated the living space from the kitchen.

"Welcome to your new home, princess."

Chapter Eleven

Cherry

"I am jealous." Zack said, throwing open the French doors that led out to my own private terrace. There was a small, heated pool and a grassy area set aside for grilling and lounging. "Really fucking jealous."

Damon just laughed, taking a sip from his drink where he sat on a barstool at the kitchen counter.

"There is an open penthouse a few doors down. I'm sure Dimitri would give you a great price on it if you asked."

Zack whipped around, a glare on his boyish features. "A great price? She gets to live here for free!"

"Calm down, boys. I'm working on convincing Dimitri to let me pay him…"

"No chance, sweetheart. He knows what happened with school and he wanted to look out for you, just like we do. Zack still had nearly the entirety of his funds, where you do not." Damon said, playing the big brother role he fit into so well.

I groaned, throwing my hands in the air as I walked towards the bedroom.

The place had two bedrooms, and I wasn't sure what to do with all the extra space. I didn't have much for myself, and I hadn't bothered shopping since the penthouse came with everything.

A handful of books graced the built-in bookshelf in the living room and my clothes didn't even fill a fourth of the huge walk-in closet. This place was far too big for just me.

What the hell had Dimitri been thinking?

"Zack, do we still have all our old stuff in storage?" I asked, wanting to fill the space with a bit more color. If the storage center still had the things from my new life, I can move it in.

"Yeah, we can call movers to bring everything by."

Chapter Twelve

Cherry

Things had been moving smoothly since moving into the new apartment. I spent my days filling the empty spaces and even getting a pet to keep me company.

I'd ended up deciding on a sweet little fox-faced Pomeranian from the local shelter. Why anyone would want to get rid of the cute white fluff ball had been beyond me. She was only nine months old and the sweetest little thing I'd ever seen.

"Bunny," I called in a sing-song voice, placing her fresh bowl of food on the kitchen floor. Looking at the counter, it was clear I may have gone overboard buying her things. I'd even gone as far as buying a fancy bed with an iron frame that resembled a daybed with a pink canopy overtop.

Bunny hopped along, looking like her name suggested, as she pranced into the kitchen to eat her dinner.

"I guess it's time I get everything set up for you." I smiled, bending over to pat her fluffy head before starting to set up her bed, toy box, and everything else I'd purchased.

I was now glad for the penthouse. The grass area on the terrace being the perfect place to let Bunny out to play and do her business. The surrounding walls were made of thick, 5 foot tall concrete to keep her from falling over an edge.

The penthouse was beginning to finally feel like my own, now that it wasn't just me.

Chapter Thirteen

Cherry

Hands.

They were everywhere. Holding my arms and legs. Covering my mouth as I tried to scream. Tears streamed down my face as they took turns.

I couldn't see their faces. Everything blurring as more tears fell and my throat felt sore.

Other parts were sore. Sore and wet.

I hated it. I just wanted them to stop.

Why hadn't anyone stopped them? Why was no one able to hear my muffled screams and cries? Did they not hear the sounds these men were making?

These were daddy's friends.

Did he know what they did to me when he wasn't around?

The way they touched me when he turned away.

The way they spoke to me. Calling me nasty names and saying things they had no business saying to a ten-year-old girl.

The things they did to me whenever there was another party.

A loud knocking sounded, pulling me from sleep.

Everything was blurry, and the banging continued as I wiped at my eyes. My hands came back wet with tears and shivers racked over my body as I tried to remember how to breathe through the sobs.

Just another nightmare.

The knocking grew louder, coming from the front door.

Using the sleeve on my sweater I'd gone to bed in, I wiped the tears from my face. All the while the pounding on my door was growing louder.

I made my way out of bed and to the front door. Who the hell came knocking on someone else's door in the middle of the night? A quick look at the clock on the stove flashing, saying 3:30 am in bright blue font.

I flung the door open wide, coming face to chest. The muscles rippled as my eyes tracked up towards the face of the person knocking on my door.

I wasn't expecting it to be Dimitri before me. His hand came up to wipe the remaining tears from my cheek. All thoughts and words leaving me as his warm skin made contact with mine.

"You were screaming," his voice was raspy from sleep. Hair uncharacteristically disheveled.

"Nightmare," was all I could say as my eyes tracked back down his chest, to that sexy as hell V that disappeared into a pair of plaid pajama pants.

A blush heated my cheeks as I noticed the outline of what he was packing beneath those pants. My eyes shooting back up to meet his ocean blue eyes.

Without any warning, he scooped me up in his arms, carrying me back into the penthouse, and kicking the door closed.

Bunny came bounding down the hall at the sound. Her little high-pitched barks followed us into the living room where he sat me on the couch.

Bunny leapt up with us, snuggling into my arms and licking the salty tears left from my nightmare.

When Dimitri was sure I was settled, petting my small dog, he made his way into the kitchen.

"What are you doing?" I asked, petting Bunny's head lightly. Scratching under her chin, just the way she liked.

He didn't answer me and I simply watched as he pulled a kettle from a cabinet, filled it with water, and put it on the stove. While the water heated, he pulled two black mugs from another cabinet and placed two tea bags into them.

"Are you making tea?" A smile tugged at my lips, chasing away the lingering feelings from the nightmare.

He leaned back against the counter, crossing his arms over his broad chest. The muscles and veins on display while he arched a brow at me.

"You were screaming so loud I could hear you from my penthouse next door. The tea will help."

"So domesticated," I grumbled, turning back to look at Bunny.

Bunny settled quickly, laying down at the end of the couch while Dimitri finished making the tea and started a low fire in the small fireplace.

Everything was bathed in a natural glow of the fire as Dimitri sat down next to me on the couch. His arm wrapped around my shoulder to pull me closer to his side. The arm around me was protective and soothing as we sipped on our tea in a companionable silence.

With him here with me, the memories had drifted back into the box they stayed hidden in and I could relax.

"The tea helps. Thank you." I whispered, the *thump, thump* of his heart allowing me to rest comfortably.

I felt him take the mug from my hand, sitting it on the table as my eyes drifted closed. His fingers lightly running through my hair. His other hand reaching into his pocket to pull out his phone. I watched in silence as he opened up his reading app and began reading wherever he'd left off.

"What are you reading now?" I asked through a yawn.

"Tolkin."

I smiled, knowing exactly who he mentioned. "Can you read some to me? Like in the old days?"

His smooth voice read the words on the page. The deep tenor rumbling his chest where I rested my head listening to the tales of Bilbo and the ring. How the fellowship was formed, and when they set off on their adventure to save middle earth.

The sound of his voice lulling me into the most peaceful sleep I'd had in weeks.

I was safe.

Chapter Fourteen

Cherry

I was so fucking late.

Rushing around the penthouse I made sure I had everything and that Bunny would be fine on her own while I was at work.

It was my first day back and I wanted to make sure that I got back on time. Damon was my best friend and I wouldn't be one of those people who took advantage of his generosity. He'd done enough for me my entire life.

That nightmare last night had really fucked with my head. They'd been happening more frequently, but that one had felt more real than the others. It had been a long time since I'd woken up actually screaming. I almost believed that I'd dreamed of Dimitri coming over too. The two mugs on the drying rack when I woke up said otherwise.

My cheeks heated at the memory of the night before and I had to shake my head to focus. Dimitri stayed with me, reading aloud to soothe me to sleep. Leaving at some time in the early morning and leaving me curled on the couch with Bunny under a blush colored throw blanket.

With a final pet to Bunny's fluffy head I ran out the door.

It had been weeks. The nightmares continued and Dimitri came in the middle of the night to stay with me while I fell back to sleep. Reading through the first two books of *The Lord of the Rings*. At this point I'd just given him my extra key to let himself inside.

Most nights he climbed into bed with me, wrapping a strong arm around me. Just having him there was a comfort. But there was one downside. My heart ached every morning when I woke to an empty bed. The bed where he'd been the night before cold.

We never talked about what kept happening and a part of me began to feel guilty for taking up so much of his time and causing him to lose sleep, even though he assured me he didn't sleep much anyways.

Today I would start seeing a therapist. Hoping to make my life and Dimitri's easier. I couldn't rely on him for comfort forever. We were barely friends and I wasn't his responsibility.

My fingers twisted the strap of my bag nervously as I sat across from the therapist, Dr. Shelby, word vomiting everything that had happened recently. From being assaulted as a child, leaving the details as vague as possible, to the incident with my professor at school, and to the guy at the club.

"So these nightmares are memories of your past?" I nodded at the question. "It seems like the incident at the club had an effect, along with all the other stresses in your life. If you are comfortable, I would like to give you a prescription for sleeping aids along with a weekly session. In the meantime, if the dreams continue, write down what happens in them so that we may discuss if there is a possible underlying concern that's causing them to reappear."

"Will the sleep aids have any side effects that interrupt my life?"

"No, they will simply help you relax at night after work and help you rest without the nightmares. We can give them a try. If you feel they are not helping or causing issues, we can look into other alternatives."

My fingers relaxed their tugging on the strap on my bag as we continued our hour-long session. The doctor asked me an array of questions and allowed me to talk though more details of my life.

After leaving her office, I felt lighter. Slipping the bottle of sleeping pills into my bag and taking a deep breath of fresh air. Begging the walk to the club before things opened up for the night.

I'd never talked to anyone about the details of my past other than Zack and Damon. They'd been my protector when I'd finally spoken up about what happened at parties.

Zack had experienced something similar, using the excuse of going over to Damon's as a way of protecting himself. Had he known the same had happened to me he would have taken me along.

He had blamed himself for that for a long time, taking me along to Damon's to escape the hell that took over what used to be our home.

Things only got worse after our mother died of an overdose when we were fifteen. At that point, we may have just been living with Damon.

He'd become our shield and protector. Willing to bloody up anyone wishing us harm. He was fifteen years older than us and took us in when we had no one else. Becoming the only reason we'd survived the next years under our father's thumb. He'd become the big brother we needed.

I would never be able to pay him or Dimitri back for all they had done for me and my idiot brother.

Chapter Fifteen

Dimitri

For the first time in weeks, I awoke to a familiar room before my alarms could go off. Glancing at the clock on my bedside table, the clock read 3:30am in a large white font.

I was usually waking up this early in an unfamiliar bed, my arms wrapped around the compact frame of a girl who smelled of fresh cherry blossoms on a warm spring day.

Today the bed felt empty, lacking that soothing aroma of the girl I'd craved my entire life, even when I had no business doing so. She must have finally slept through the night.

With a groan, I pulled myself from the bed and slipped into a pair of grey sweatpants. Every morning I woke up early to get a workout in before work. Having woken up early I could complete my usual routine and still have a moment to go check on her.

Heading downstairs to the gym, I completed a quick full-body workout. Followed by showering, getting ready for the day, and setting the expensive as hell coffee machine to brew two cups of coffee as I finished getting ready.

Not bothering with my tie, simply slipping it around my neck for later, I grabbed the mugs and headed next door.

Letting myself in, I was greeted at the door by the little fur ball Cherry insisted was a dog. Letting the thing outside, I left the door open for it to roam back in while I made my way to Chery's room.

Stopping short in the doorway, I couldn't help but stare. For the first time that I'd seen her sleeping, she seemed peaceful. No worry creasing her brown or her lips turned down in a frown.

No, this relaxed Cherry was a sight to behold. Looking angelic as her golden hair fanned around her pretty heart-shaped face. If I'd been the smiling type, I may have done so now. Instead, my face stayed neutral as I glanced around the room, noticing a small orange bottle next to the bed.

Setting the mugs on the bedside table, I picked up the bottle to inspect it. Prazosin was written against the label and I pulled my phone out to see what it was for.

My brows creased as I read an article full of information on how it was a sleeping aid used to treat PTSD-associated nightmares.

While I didn't know the details of what she had faced in her youth, I knew she had suffered at the hand of her asshole father and drug addict mother. It had been the reason for the Vahn twins living with us for the final years before gaining their inheritance.

Could her dreams have been about whatever had happened back then? Old demons come to bring her down during a stressful time in her life?

It wasn't my place to ask questions about her personal life. She wasn't mine, though at times I wished she was.

Placing the bottle and my phone onto the nightstand, I moved to brush the stray hair from her innocent face. Her eyes fluttered as I slid my fingers down her smooth cheek.

"Dimitri," she sighed out my name, sounding content as those jade green eyes met mine.

How I wished she were saying my name as she found her pleasure. The thought sending a jolt of need to my straining cock. The length pressed into the zipper of my slacks.

"You slept through the night, princess. I came to check on you and brought coffee."

A yawn spilled from her as she stretched. Arching her back off the bed, her low cut sleeping shirt giving me a generous view of her hardened nipples under the silk fabric.

Fuck, this woman would be the death of me.

As discreetly as possible, I adjusted myself, reaching to hand her one of the mugs. She sat up in her bed, took the mug into her hands, before taking a long sip of the steaming liquid.

"I needed this." She moaned with a sign. "Thank you for the coffee and for coming to check on me."

Her green eyes shone bright as she looked at me and I had to look away, clearing my throat.

"I actually need a favor." I stated, sounding bored as I stood. Walking over to her floor-length mirror to tie the tie hanging loosely around my neck.

I didn't look as I heard her sit down her mug and her soft footsteps walking towards me.

No longer looking at my face as she reached for the ends of the tie from my hands, turning me to face her once more as she finished tying the black fabric.

"Ask." Her voice was soft as my eyes looked down on her smaller frame. I really was much taller than her. Her 5'2" frame coming to rest at chest level to my 6'3". She was so small, driving me to want to protect her. She'd always seemed so innocent despite what she went through. The girl I knew growing into the strong, beautiful woman before me.

No, that was simply my own desire to protect her. I wanted her. Wanted to make her mine in every way. To protect her from this shit world, we were forced to be a part of because of who our families were. But she deserved better than a bastard like me.

"I need a date for a charity auction Friday night."

Her fingers paused before she quickly finished tying the fabric around my neck. Hands sliding down to rest on my chest as that hypnotizing gaze met my icy stare. A light pink covering her pale cheeks.

Chapter Sixteen

Cherry

I still couldn't wrap my head around the fact Dimitri had asked me to be his date tonight. It had been 4 days since he'd asked. That alone had me in a panic since the moment he'd left, and I realized I'd said yes. My heart leapt for joy while my head made it clear this wasn't an actual date. It was probably just something last minute and his usual dates were busy. It didn't mean anything.

The panic only intensified as I went through the gowns I owned, looking for the perfect one. The selection was embarrassingly limited.

After leaving this place, I'd sold almost every gown I owned, leaving only two options for me now.

I never intended to need them again. One was a strapless, powder blue mermaid style dress. It was simple, with only the tulle overlay on the skirt.

The second choice was one I'd never had a chance to wear. It was a full ball gown in a light rose-gold color. The bodice was fitted, made of a nearly glitter fabric in a halter top style with a plunging neckline that dropped to the top of my navel. Leaf-like shapes made of an ivory shape wrapped around the sides. It was completely backless, which showed off my cherry blossom tree tattoo that took up most of my back. The skirt was a thin material that was covered in layer upon layer of pink champagne tulle that pooled around my legs and fell back into a short train. The leaf and floral pattern embroidered to continue down the lengths of the skirt.

It was elegant, modern, and the pink color made my pale skin appear to glow with warmth.

"This one." I smiled while laying the rose-gold and champagne dress on the bed while I went to shower. Everything tonight had to be perfect. The last thing I wanted was to be an embarrassment to Dimitri in front of what I was sure would be the elite class of the city.

I did a simple nude makeup look with a rosy pink lipstick to compliment the pinks in the dress. Curling my hair to add some extra volume, leaving it half down so that it cascaded down between my shoulders and a simple bun to hold up the rest. Keeping the stands from falling into my face during the night. Small face framing pieces were the only thing kept at the sides of my face. It was much more put together than my usual grunge look.

The overall look was soft as I looked myself over in the floor-length mirror. The dress showed off a bit more skin than I was used to as I spun to see it from every angle.

A quick glance at my phone showed I had just enough time to slip on my shoes and grab my rose-gold clutch before Dimitri was supposed to be here. Whatever made me save this outfit was a godsend. I just hoped that Dimitri approved.

Rushing to the bed, I piled the skirt of the dress up in my arms in an attempt to slid on the strappy nude heels I'd picked out for the night.

"Come on," I groaned as I struggled to get the strap wrapped around my ankle and buckled.

I must have struggled longer than I'd planned as I heard the front door open and Bunny's excited yips and nails tapping on the hardwood floors. The fact she was so excited made it clear who it was coming into the apartment.

"I'm in the room finishing up Dimitri." I yelled out, still struggling with the damned shoe.

A sigh of frustration left me as I tossed the offending thing onto the floor. At the same instance Dimitri's form filled my bedroom doorway.

My breath hitched as I took him in, leaning against the doorframe as his eyes appraised me. Scanning from my face down to where my skirt was still pulled up around my waist, then landing on the heel thrown to the floor.

My eyes trailing from his perfectly styled dark brown hair, clean shaven stern facial features, to his all black tux. The man was a god among men and I was nearly salivating, forcing my gaze back to those piercing ocean eyes. Eyes that were still tracking over every inch of me. I could have sworn they even darkened as he looked me over. Something flashing over his features that I couldn't exactly read. Like an animal who'd just found his prey. But that had to be my imagination.

Dimitri said nothing as he strolled into the room, taking a knee in front of me and picking up my discarded shoe. Hand trailing down my calf to my ankle as he slipped the heel onto my foot. He buckled the strap with ease, moving to the other foot with the same fluid motions until my shoes were firmly in place as a heat engulfed my cheeks and core.

A man, Dimitri of all people, putting on my shoes had no business being so erotic. A burning need rushed through me as I imagined those hands sliding further up my legs.

He stood, exuding the same fluid grace and confidence he always carried. He offered me a hand, which I took to stand. Even in five-inch heels, he seemed to tower over me. Maybe it was that he was actually much taller than me, or maybe it was the way he carried himself.

"Thank you." I whispered, watching his eyes take me in once more.

"You look beautiful, princess." His voice sounded husky and deeper than normal before he pulled me from the room to the front door.

My god, my face would melt off from the blush that had taken over me. I was heated in all the best, and worst ways as he led me from my apartment.

Glancing back as the door closed, I saw Bunny jump onto the couch and curl into her blanket for the night.

Dimitri taking care to carefully lock up before leading me to the elevator.

Tonight was turning into something I never would have expected as Dimitri's fingers interlaced with mine.

Chapter Seventeen

Dimitri

This may have been the worst and best decision I'd ever made in my life. I couldn't take my eyes off her as we made our way around the auction.

Seeing her sitting on her bed, the skirts of her dress pulled up to show the long, creamy legs underneath as she struggled to put on her shoes. I had the image of those same legs wrapped around my waist as I brought her pleasure. Fantasizing about how she would taste on my tongue as I consumed her. Imagined the sounds she would make for me as I made her come until she was spent.

For now, I took my time watching her. While it had been awhile since Cherry had been a part of this world, she fit back into the society with ease. Her dress flowed around her as we mingled with the other business owners, elected officials, and wealthy class that was in attendance this evening.

Watching her was like watching a goddess among mortals. Conversing with the foolish mortals who should worship the ground at her feet. The Persephone to my Hades. In that damned dress she truly looked the part of the goddess of spring from the old tales. Books and stories I'd loved reading as a child.

She was currently talking to a senator and his wife as they spoke about the city and welcomed her back to finer society.

A slower song playing from the band that was in attendance, entertaining for tonight's event. Turning modern songs into instrumental ballads as couples danced within the large dance space in the center of the room. Tables surrounding the walls with an array of items to bid on.

Tonight's auction was to help the children less fortunate in our city. Orphans, homeless, and displaced families that did not have the needed resources to live a decent life. Something that had been a big focus of mine with the company. A way to make up for the shady business deals my father was a part of. The more children I could save, the less there would be for him to make a profit from.

Cherry's hand slid back into mine as she wished the senator and his wife well.

"It was nice seeing you, sweetheart. I will be in touch." The senator's wife said, placing a kiss on Cherry's cheek before they walked off.

"Making connections, princess?" I asked, walking her over to the refreshments table.

"I'm not sure I want to be a waitress for the rest of my life. No offense to your brother. I do appreciate what he's done for me, but I had other plans that didn't work out so well. Marsha runs a charity that helps youth in the city. They are looking for volunteer counselors and maybe I could be of some help on the days I'm not working at Hellfire."

Her eyes held a dreamy look, with a far off expression as she spoke. Helping people, especially children, seemed to be something she strived towards. I still wasn't aware of the details of why she'd ended up here.

Something about an affair with a professor and being asked to leave the school before finishing her degree.

I wanted to know more, but it wasn't my place to push. If she wanted to tell me why she'd come back to this city, she could tell me in her own time. It wasn't my place to pry into her life when I had no right. She wasn't mine.

I handed her another flute of champagne. Setting her empty glass to the side. "No matter what you may have faced, it is admirable that you still want to help others."

"Well, of course! Not everyone has someone to help them, like Zack and I did. We were lucky to have Damon and you close by."

I nodded in understanding. I'd done very little to help the twins back then. Keeping my distance and only ensuring they had the financial means for whatever they needed until they were old enough to gain their inheritance. Their father was just as much of a shit bag as my father. Sticking their hands into the same pot of filth in this city's underground just to earn more than they needed. They hadn't cared who they hurt, so long as it lined their pockets.

We walked around the room, Cherry on my arm as we placed bids on unique items. It was all set up as a silent auction. No one knowing until after the event who won which items with their donations.

Her hand felt light on my arm as she looked over each item, lighting up when she saw a unique sort of pink diamond ring that was up for auction. A larger pink stone shaped like an oval, encased in rose gold and surrounded by a halo of white diamonds in what appeared to be a floral design. The small white diamonds moving to wrap around the band. It was elegant and sophisticated, with a touch of wonder. The perfect ring to match the gown this goddess on my arm wore tonight.

When her attention moved to look at something else on display, I placed a bid on the ring. The light that shone in her eye when she looked at it was worth every damn penny.

"If it isn't my so-called daughter." Came a gruff, older voice from behind us. Cherry's hand tightening on my arm as we turned to face the old fuck.

Chapter Eighteen

Cherry

My blood ran cold at the voice behind us. My hand tightening on Dimitri's arm.

What the hell was he doing here?

We turned to face my father. Dimitri's hand gave mine a small squeeze before going to rest protectively around my waist.

My father's short, round frame and balding head I'd been expecting, but not the man standing next to him.

"Jackson." His name left my lips in a whisper as I took in his put together appearance. Pepper hair slicked back, almost effortlessly. His entrancing hazel eyes watching my every move, his face covered in a well groomed short beard, and his usual charismatic smile beaming. His eyes fell to rest on Dimitri's hand around my waist where he pulled me closer.

"It's nice to finally see you again, Cherry." Jackson stepped forward, gripped my hand to pull me away from Dimitri's side. Placing a light kiss on my knuckles as he looked up at me. Anger and need mixing in his hazel eyes.

The familiar scruff of that beard sent waves of nausea through my system, so unlike how I'd used to feel at his touch. A touch that I used to crave turned to one of disgust. I heard Dimitri calmly clear his throat, giving me the opportunity to pull my hand away from Jackson without appearing disrespectful. Taking a step back towards Dimitri's side.

"And who might you be?" Dimitri asked, his ocean blues tracking over Jackson as if he were calculating where to best land his first hit. His hand extended to clasp Jackson's in a much firmer grip than necessary.

Dimitri's suits and pretty words had never fooled me. He might be the businessman of the Ashford brothers, but he was never scared to get his hands dirty. Dimitri could be just as ruthless as Damon. He was a dangerous man, and I felt safer as he pulled me back into his side. Our bodies pressed together perfectly, fitting together like two puzzle pieces. Like we were made for each other. It was his way of claiming me publically. All while protecting me from the two men before us.

"Oh, Cherry hasn't talked about me?" Jackson asked, sounding surprised as he placed a hand on his chest as if he were wounded.

"No," was all Dimitri said, never glancing in my direction as he faced off with my ex. Completely in control and showing no signs of worry. He was the one in charge of this small gathering. The leader and it oozed from every pore.

"Well, I'm Jackson Stewart, Cherry's boyfriend and psychology professor from the university."

"Ex," I said under my breath. Jackson sounded proud of himself and I wanted to knock him down a peg. I wasn't interested in anything he had to say. He'd lost any chance of us working after everything that had happened.

Dimitri's hand pulled me closer. "Apparently, you two see your relationship in a different light. Cherry is no longer your concern."

"On the contrary," my father spoke up, pushing his way into the heated standoff between these two. "I have been speaking with Jackson, and it is in the best interest of the family that you two be together. Cherry will complete her education, which I've so graciously paid for these past years, and all that nonsense with the school can be swept under the rug. A marriage will work wonders for everyone involved."

I nearly stopped breathing, feeling the burn of tears in the backs of my eyes. I pushed them back, not willing to give either of them the satisfaction. There was no way my father actually believed an arranged marriage would work in this situation. Had that been why he'd been trying to contact me? Had he been looking for a way to keep any sort of scandal regarding my expulsion from the school under wraps?

While arranged marriage was always a possibility in this world of riches we lived in, it was usually frowned upon. Only used in instances to gain strength and bonds with others.

"No." Dimitri said, his hand slipping back into mine as he pulled me away from the two men before us. "If you will excuse us, I would like to dance with my date."

He gave them no other farewell, pulling me towards the dance floor as *Half Life by Livingston* began to play from the band. It made me think of the *Bridgerton* show with the way the music was given a romantic edge with a mix of classical instruments. Dimitri showing expert skill as he twirled me into the middle of the throng of people dancing as we began a slow, elegant dance.

"Just focus on me," he whispered in a deep tenor against the shell of my ear as he pulled me close. One hand sliding to my waist while he held the other, leading us into an elaborate dance. Twirling me at the perfect moments and holding me close the rest of the time as we glided across the floor. I was beyond thankful that the train of this dress was short enough that I'd been able to slip the strap to my wrist. Leaving me plenty of space in the skirt to follow Dimitri's lead.

The warmth of his embrace sent shivers up my back and caused a calm to settle over me. My father could broker a proposal all he wanted, but he had no say in what

I actually did with my life. I had gut ties with him and my family name years ago.

I wouldn't worry about that right now. Choosing to just focus on the firm hand on my waist as we danced to the music. Dimitri twirling me until I was dizzy, and a smile played on my lips.

"Thank you."

"There is nothing to thank me for. Just enjoy tonight with me, princess. I won't let anything happen to you." His words sent warmth to my chest.

He didn't have to do any of this.

One dance led to another and another until I was nearly delirious with happiness filling my chest. I even saw a smirk gracing Dimitri's stern face from time to time as we talked and spun around the dance floor.

"Have I told you tonight that you look stunning? Like the goddess of spring." His words tickled across my lips as he held me close, ocean eyes staring into my very soul.

This was the second time he'd been so close, and all I wanted was to close the gap between us. To press my lips to his and see if there was a spark of anything between us. To see if he wanted the same things I did.

"No." I whispered, slipping my hand from his shoulder to toy with his tie, dropping my eyes to his lips. All I wanted was to yank him to me. To close the distance, but I wouldn't make the first move. I needed to know he wanted this. Wanted me. I wanted him so badly I ached for any sort of contact.

"My apologies." His eyes dropped to my lips, the distance seeming to shrink between us as the rest of the room blurred out of focus, as if we were in our own world. Like we were the only two people in the room.

"Dimitri," His name left my lips, sounding like a prayer.

"Fuck." The word came out gruff before he closed the distance between us. Somehow, his hand left mine to slip into my hair, deepening the kiss as I clung to his jacket for balance. My world turned on its axis as everything seemed to fall into place. A fire consumed me until I felt dizzy and scorched under its heat wave.

Tonight felt like the start of something life altering and I didn't want it to ever end.

Chapter Nineteen

Cherry

How we ended up back in the limo and back to the apartments was a complete blur. All I could focus on was the feel of Dimitri's hands and mouth on me. Taking from me until I was a needy mess. Hating the feeling of our clothes in the way of anything else happening.

I wanted more as he unlocked his apartment door without breaking the hungry kiss we shared.

As soon as the door was open, he picked me up, my legs going around his waist on instinct as he carried us inside. The skirt of the damned dress gathered between us. Kicking the door closed before pressing my back against the wall, one hand moving from my waist to push the layers of skirt from my legs. His hand sliding up my thigh to delve to my core. Every caress of his fingers causing goosebumps in their wake as his fingers moved up further until he reached the aching part of me.

"Cherry," He groaned my name against my lips, finding that I was bare underneath my dress. His fingers sliding against my slick entrance.

My hands fisted in his hair, deepening the kiss as I moaned. His fingers found my clit and worked me in slow circles. The sounds of how wet I was mingling with our panting breaths and moans of pleasure.

Lips trailed from mine, along my jaw, and down my neck as he slipped a finger into my heated center. Quickly adding a second, as his palm moved to give me the friction I needed.

"So wet for me, princess." His teeth sank into the skin where my neck and shoulder met, sucking until I was sure there would be marks on my flesh in the morning.

"Dimitri. More, please." I begged. I needed more than this slow tease. The rational side of my brain was screaming that we needed to stop, but my heart and body wanted more.

It didn't take anymore begging on my part. Something in Dimitri wanted this just as much as I did. His fingers slipping from my core. A whimper of protect leaving me at the loss of his touch. Until I heard the sound of a zipper before I felt his hard length pressing against me.

I moaned at the feeling as he slipped the tip against my wet folds before plunging in with one effortless thrust.

Something in me snapped as he bottomed out inside me and I moaned out his name, my head falling back against the wall as he began to thrust in and out of me. My walls clenching around his massive size as he took everything I had to offer.

"Oh god, right there." My voice was husky with pleasure as he fucked me, filling me until I was sure I'd be split in two.

"I am the only god you will ever cry out to, princess." He growled, lips finding mine as his hands gripped my thighs, pressing me harder into the wall.

All I could do was take what he gave me. Until the waves of pleasure crashed over me. Fisting his hair in a white knuckle grip as he fucked me through my orgasm. Drawing out every ounce of ecstasy from me.

"That's it princess, come on my cock like the good girl you are." His words only heightening the pleasure coursing through me.

"Please," I begged though I wasn't sure what I was even begging for.

His lips found mine again as he pushed inside me one more time. Hands holding me wrapped around him as he moved us from the wall and walked down the hall into the bedroom.

A whimper leaving me as he pulled from me, laying me on the bed, my dress pooling around me. His hands never leaving my thighs as he sank to his knees between my spread legs. A groan left me as I felt his tongue slide up my center.

A growl came from him as he tasted me. "Mine."

That single word vibrated through me before he dove his tongue into me for a deeper taste.

"So fucking sweet." Another lick up to my clit where he flattened his tongue.

My hips lifting from the bed to chase the feeling. All I could do was grab fistfuls of fabric as he doubled his efforts, any teasing gone as he devoured me. The sounds leaving me loud and obscene. I'd never been so vocal, but the things his tongue was doing to me were unlike anything I'd ever experienced before. No one had ever tasted me and from the sounds he was making against me he seemed to be enjoying it just as much.

When the next orgasm hit me, I was shamelessly grinding against his mouth.

"Oh, yes, Dimitri, fuck, fuck, fuck."

He licked me until I was breathless, legs shaking from so many climaxes back to back. A blush creeped over my cheeks as he stood, laying himself atop me. His lips found mine as his still hard erection pressed against my soaked pussy.

I could taste myself in this kiss, causing another moan to leave me. Everything he did seeming so erotic. At the sound, Dimitri took the chance to slip his tongue into my mouth. Tongues tangling as he ground himself against my sensitive flesh. The length of his cock sliding against my sex just right until I could feel that wave building higher still.

He broke the kiss, leaving me cold in his absence, never slowing the movements of his hips. "I'm not finished with you yet, princess."

Chapter Twenty

Dimitri

This woman would be the death of me.

I wanted to taste her. To fuck her. To make her mine in every way as I looked down at her sprawled on my bed. Her golden waves fanned around her like a halo. Face flushed and green eyes dark with desire. The pink skirt of her dress bunched around her waist. Legs still spread wide, giving me the perfect view of her swollen and glistening cunt as I rubbed my length against her.

She was a goddess, opening herself up to my worship and worship her I would. I would fuck her so thoroughly that she would never be fulfilled by another. She'd crave me. Her own personal addiction that only I could fill.

I'd make her mine.

I would make her beg for all of me. For every depraved thing I wanted to do to her and she would enjoy every second of it.

"Stand up, I want to see all of you princess." I stood back, giving her room to stand from the bed on shaking legs. Her skirt falling back into place to brush the ground at her feet. Eyes watching me, full of questions.

"Undress." I ordered, moving to lean against the dresser. My hand wrapping around my throbbing cock.

She didn't fight or talk back. Something I liked about her. We would have to talk if she wanted to continue this after tonight. I needed to make sure she was safe and comfortable with everything I wanted from her.

Moving to unzip the dress, she slipped the straps from her shoulders, letting the fabric fall around her feet. Eyes never leaving the hand working my dick slowly as I watched her. Her pink tongue licking her lips as she watched my fist working. She stepped from the fabric in nothing but those nude strappy heels.

"Leave those on," I said, nodding towards the shoes. "Now crawl to me."

Shock making her eyes blow wide, "what?"

Her voice sounded like a squeak as her eyes flew up to meet mine. "Crawl. To. Me." I punctuated each word with a tight fisted stroke of my cock, pre-cum leaking from the tip.

She paused for only a second longer before moving to the floor. Hands and knees moving over the hardwood as she crawled to me. Hips swaying in a manner that made me groan in pleasure. If I had any less control, I could come just from that view.

"Such a good girl. You look so beautiful on your knees for me." I moved my hand faster, veins straining against the skin as pleasure raced through me.

When she was before me, I pressed my cock in her direction. Running the glistening tip against those pretty pink lips of hers. "Suck."

There was no complaint as she opened wide for me, taking the head of my cock between her warm, pink lips. The lipstick she wore tonight already smeared on her pretty face from our kissing, making me throb.

I'd never been so hard in my life as I moved my hand from my length for her to take completely. Lips sliding down my cock slowly as she swirled her tongue on the way down. Cheeks hollowed as she sucked, taking me from root to tip at a slow pace that drove me insane. Hands moving to her tangled locks, fighting the urge to simply use her. To fuck her mouth like a beast. But I needed her to enjoy this. I wouldn't simply take from her.

This had to be right.

"That's it, princess. Look at you taking my cock so well." The praise spurred her on, the pace quickening as she took me deeper into her throat, a moan slipping from her to vibrate against me.

"I'm going to fuck that pretty mouth now. If you need to stop, tap my leg three times." As soon as the words left me, I was gripping her head and plunging deep into her warm mouth. Fucking her roughly until tears and mascara slid down her cheeks.

Her hands found my thighs, nails digging into the fabric of my tuxedo pants. There was something about being fully clothed while she was on her knees, completely exposed to me. It made me feel powerful.

I groaned out her name in pleasure, feeling my balls drawing up. Fuck, she felt far too good wrapped around my cock.

"Touch yourself, princess." I growled, moving my hips faster, chasing my own release.

I watched as she looked up at me through long, wet lashes. One hand moving from my leg to plunge between her parted thighs. As her fingers slid against her folds, I could hear the slick sounds of her fingers moving in and out of her perfect pussy.

"So fucking wet for me. Now make yourself come while I fuck that pretty face."

Her fingers moved faster, hips rolling against her hand as she worked herself to the same punishing pace that I used to fuck her mouth. Her lips tightening around me the closer she got to her release. The wet sounds and our moans of pleasure filled the dark room as we raced towards complete ecstasy.

I watched as she crashed over the edge of pleasure, a loud moan working through my groin as her eyes rolled back.

With a final, hard thrust down her slender throat I came. Shooting ropes of come into her waiting mouth. Her name left me as a groan while she swallowed around me.

When I was spent, I pulled from her pink lips, slipping my hand to cup her face. Her eyes were filled with tears, gasps leaving her rapidly as her breast bounced with every deep breath she took.

"So perfect." I praised, offering her a hand to stand.

Chapter Twenty-One

Cherry

I'd thought that once he'd come in my mouth, it would be the end of whatever this was. But Dimitri had surprised me. He'd helped me stand before undressing completely and leading me back to the bed. His dick was still hard as he lay in the bed behind me.

He had wrapped his arms around me, filling me up from behind as he fucked me until I was soaking his cock and sheets.

Still not finished until he'd made me come three more times. Coming inside me and then using his fingers to push his spend back into my core until I came on his hand.

I'd been boneless, my mind foggy with pleasure as he cleaned us both up and climbed back into the bed with me. Pulling me into his warm embrace until I fell into a deep sleep.

I wouldn't have believed any of the night before had happened if it hadn't been for waking up wrapped in Dimitri's arms. He'd pulled me closer the moment I stirred, face buried in my hair as I relaxed further into his hold.

He'd left for a workout about an hour ago and left me to wander his penthouse. It was a lot like mine. I'd taken the time to go grab Bunny from my apartment while he'd been gone. She was currently lounging on the couch while I was finishing up making breakfast for when Dimitri was back. He didn't have work today and wanted me to stay here.

I hadn't been expecting to stay around. Thinking that last night was only a one time thing. In the years I'd known Dimitri, he'd never kept anyone around long.

At the thought of last night, I couldn't imagine working out after last night. I was sore in all the best places. Bruised finger prints on my waist and thighs, hickies on my lower neck and shoulders. I looked a mess after my shower, but had never felt so light in my life.

My fingers lightly tracing where the deepest purple marks that graced my skin. I didn't mind the marks. They made me feel cared for. The feeling of completeness filling my chest as I hummed along to my phone's playlist.

The door opened as I placed the last egg on a plate and I smiled at Dimitri's sweaty body as he toweled off his damp hair with a towel wrapped around his shoulders. He was shirtless, showing off his toned muscles and his grey sweatpants hanging low on his hips. The faint impression of his cock making my mouth water for another taste of him.

"Princess, if you keep looking at me like that I'll have to bend you over that counter." His voice had an edge to it as his eyes narrowed on me. Taking in the button-up shirt I'd stolen from his closet when he left. "On second thought," he rushed towards me, wrapping his arms around me to press my hips into the counter, pressing his hardening length into my backside.

"Dimitri," I gasped, dropping the plate of food onto the counter with little care. His hand reaching between our bodies in search of my throbbing center.

When his fingers slid through the evidence of my desire, he groaned, placing a soft kiss on my shoulder as he plunged a finger into me.

"This pussy is always so wet for me. Made for me." His praise washed over me, causing another moan to slip past my lips.

His other hand slid up the back of my head, gripping a fitful of hair as he pushed me forward until I was lying on the counter. With my ass in the air and toes barely touching the floor. He removed his fingers, quickly pushing his pants down to free his cock. Filling me in one thrust, my core clenching around him. That ache that had been left from last night shifting to one of pleasure. His hand moved between us to rub at my swollen clit while he plunged into me from behind.

This fucking was quick, sending me over the edge in a matter of moments until I could feel the evidence of my orgasm running down my legs.

"Fuck, more Dimitri." I was a mess of want as he plowed into me. The wet sounds of our fucking mingling with the music still playing on my phone.

The hand in my hair yanked my head back, pulling on the scalp and causing a whimper to leave me. "Say please, princess."

His words sounded husky with his own desire, thrusts becoming slow and languid. Teasing me until all I could do was beg for more.

"Please, sir." The words fell from me, seeming to shock us both for a moment until he thrust into me harder. Each thrust came faster than the last as I was pushed closer and closer to another orgasm.

"Again."

"Fuck! Fuck me harder, sir." I groaned at his relentless pace. The slip of the word spurring him on until we were both delirious. This stoic man letting loose like some untamed beast, while all I could do was take his beautiful abuses. One orgasm crested into another until I lost count. My legs felt like jello and a slew of words leaving me in guttural groans of pleasure. Any words I said were jumbled and hard to understand, as my world seemed to tilt. A place where I couldn't even remember my own name. The only thing that mattered was the feeling of this man inside me.

"Oh god, right there, please don't stop."

He fucked me until my toes no longer touched the floor and the counter dug into my hips, but I didn't care. All I could care about was the feeling of him twitching inside me as we both found our releases with the moan of each other's names.

He held himself inside me as we both fought to catch our breath. Whatever had taken over in those moments of passion fading away. Leaving us both panting and sated.

"That was..."

There wasn't a word to describe what had just happened. My face heated from what I'd called him while in a heated moment. That had been what his father made us all refer to him as while growing up. I wasn't sure how he would take it, especially now that we were getting back to normal. The haze of lust fading with every passing second. Something like that had never happened before and I wasn't sure what would happen now after all the sex had ended.

Dimitri pulled from me, reaching for the kitchen towel to clean us both up from the mess we'd made.

"Do you want to talk about it?" He asked, turning me to face him, a stern look on his handsome face.

I still hadn't found my words, so I shook my head. He didn't push the subject, though I noticed worry creasing his brow. Instead of asking again he only placed a kiss on my forehead before moving to throw the towel in the laundry room and reheat our now cold breakfast.

We ate in silence, the only nose Bunny's nails on the floor as she pranced and yelped, begging Dimitri for another piece of egg or bacon.

"You're going to spoil her if you keep feeding her from your plate." I said, raising a brow at him.

He paid me no mind, tossing another small piece of egg that Bunny caught in mid-air. Her tail wagged happily as she looked up at him.

I rolled my eyes, a smile on my face as I finished up my breakfast. This all felt perfect and right. Like we were just meant to fit into each other's lives. I would happily spend every day like this.

Chapter Twenty-Two

Cherry

Things had moved along fast.

It had been nearly a week since the charity ball and Dimitri had taken to staying in my apartment on the nights I wasn't working at Hellfire.

Nothing had been made *official* between us, but it felt like the most natural thing to be together. I had no reservations that this was a simple fling, since Dimitri had told Damon about us. It wasn't a situation like with Jackson where we had to keep things secret. Dimitri wanted me to be his, but I was a bit more reserved. Not sure I wanted news getting back to my father or Jackson.

A part of me was also scared that everything was too good to be true. That I was just waiting for the other shoe to drop or Dimitri to get tired of me.

Every day now, there had been a delivery of some kind. Flowers and jewelry delivered with notes from Jackson. All stating how we needed to talk. How he couldn't wait for me to be his wife, ready to put the past behind us and move on together.

His number, along with my father's, was still blocked. How they'd known where I lived still worried me, but Dimitri had taken the time to set up a state-of-the-art security system in both our apartments to be safe.

Currently, my idiot twin was making fun of me while pouring a glass of whiskey for a customer.

"Does he have to sit over there and watch you work? It's kinda weird, sis." Zack tilted his head towards one of the VIP areas, towards where Dimitri was talking with some business partners over drinks. His eyes never leaving me even while conversing with the other men around him.

"Something about wanting me safe." I shrugged, placing the last drink for my next walk around onto a tray. With the packages and notes being delivered, Dimitri was worried that Jackson would try to get to me at work. He and Damon made sure that an image of Jackson, showing him as black listed, was shown to all the bouncers at Hellfire.

I wasn't sure that it was a valuable use of resources, but having Dimitri around did make me feel safer, from handsy customers and Jackson. From my experience, Jackson was harmless. Even if my father had gotten to him I didn't see a need for my being watched. But something had gotten under Dimitri's skin the night of the auction. If it made him feel better to make sure I was safe, who was I to object?

The night went by quickly and I was nearly dead on my feet with how busy things had been. I'd been so tired that I'd fallen asleep in the car on the way back to the apartment. Only waking when Dimitri opened the door to help me out and to the building's elevator.

He held me close, arm wrapped around my waist as I rested my head on his chest. He led us to my apartment door, placing a kiss on my forehead.

"I need to grab a change of clothes for tomorrow and then I'll be right over."

"Okay," I smiled up at him, watching as he unlocked the door to his own apartment, disappearing inside.

I turned to my own door, unlocking the deadbolt and pushing it open to my dark apartment.

"That's odd." I thought, pretty sure I'd left the light on for Bunny when I'd left for work tonight. I must have spaced it and turned it off by accident.

Hand on the wall, I felt for the switch that turned on the lights for the kitchen and living room area of the house. Flipping the switch, the blinding lights blinked to life.

A scream of utter horror tore from me at the sight before me. Tears streamed down my face as I fell to my knees.

Chapter Twenty-Three

Dimitri

I heard the scream, and my heart lurched into my throat. Dropping everything on my closet floor, I rushed next door to Cherry's, not at all prepared for the scene before me.

Cherry knelt on the floor in a puddle of blood, sobs racking her frame as he knelt over the fluffy white form of her dog, Bunny. Her fur matted in blood, the knife still protruding from her side where she lay on the hardwood flooring.

There was blood everywhere as I made my way to Cherry, pulling her into my arms. I couldn't understand her words through the sobs as she clung to me. I didn't even think about what to do next, lifting her into my arms and taking her straight to my apartment. Sitting her on the couch, her sobs filling the quiet space.

Walking into the kitchen, already dialing the number for the police as I got to work making Cherry a glass of whiskey. Making it a double and taking the bottle back with me to the living room.

Tea wouldn't cut it tonight.

I handed her the glass, watching her down it as I ran a hand through her hair and finished up the call with the police

Kneeling in front of her, I took her tear-stained face between my hands. Looking into her beautiful green eyes that seemed void of any sort of light. It was like she wasn't even seeing me right now.

"Princess, do you need me to call someone? The police will be here soon. I can have Zack and Damon here to keep you company while I deal with everything."

She didn't speak, just nodded, and I refilled her glass, sending a quick text to my brother and friend as I took a seat next to her. Pulling her into my embrace as she downed another glass.

The sobs turned to silent tears that tumbled down her cheeks that I wiped away with a handkerchief from my jacket pocket. The pain that radiated off her made me see red as I waited for everyone to arrive. I wouldn't leave her alone like this.

When I find that bastard, I'd make him regret the day he was born. This world would burn if it needed to so that I could get my hands on him.

What was really only an hour felt like a lifetime as I spoke with the police. Handing over the videos from the security cameras of Jackson slipping through the back doors of the building and into Cherry's apartment.

He hadn't been expecting the dog who'd attacked him when he came inside. The little fur ball went after his ankle until he had picked her up by her fur and drove the knife into her small body until she no longer moved. He'd continued into the apartment, tearing the place apart before disappearing into her room. That and the bathroom being the only rooms in the penthouse that didn't have cameras.

He'd done well to hide his face, dressed in all black with a hood and ball cap. But I knew it was him. That fucker had signed his death warrant with the shit he pulled tonight.

Without a positive ID, the police were useless. This would have to be done off the books.

With a quick call to our family cleaning lady, Rosa, I got to work wrapping the poor dog in a towel. I'd take care of all of this so that Cherry didn't have to.

I couldn't stand the hurt on her face when I found her kneeling on this floor. The sound of her screams still ringing in my ears.

I'd have the dog cremated until she could decide what she wanted to do. The cleaners would make this place spotless, and after tonight Cherry would be staying with me, permanently.

I wouldn't let anything like this ever happen to her again. She'd been through enough.

Damon walked in, lighting a cigarette as I was finishing up wrapping up Bunny in the towel.

"Need anything, brother?" He asked, stuffing his hands in his jean pockets. A ring of smoke formed above his head.

"Take her somewhere they can cremate her. Cleaners are on the way." He took the wrapped bundle from my hands with a nod.

I was covered in blood. I didn't bother unbuttoning my dress shirt, simply ripping it over my head to toss in the trash and walking over to the sink to wash myself off.

"Zack is next door with Cherry. I'll take care of the pup, and Jensen is already on the hunt for the asshole. I'll give you a call when we have him." Damon said around his cigarette as he moved out of the door and disappeared down the hall.

When I was sure that everything was clean, I went into the bedroom to find Cherry's bed a rumpled mess and things strewn around the room. Glass broken and the place completely trashed. I grabbed a discarded bag, placing the things she'd need into it that didn't appear disturbed. I'd replace everything tomorrow. Get her all new bathroom utensils and new clothes. Whatever she wanted and needed.

I didn't bother locking the place as I made my way to my apartment. Some superhero movie playing on the TV as Zack sat on the couch, nursing a glass of whiskey. The bottle on the coffee table, now empty.

Cherry's head was in her brother's lap. She'd fallen asleep, tears still staining her rosy cheeks as I dropped the bag on the kitchen counter. Grabbing another bottle and a glass from the kitchen, I moved into the living room. Pouring a fresh glass for Zack before taking a seat on the couch next to the twins. Pouring a generous glass of whiskey for myself..

"You got him?" Zack asked, eyes never straying from the TV as some guy with a horned helmet fell from a flying contraption after catching an exploding arrow.

I took another swig of my drink. "I will."

"Good. I'll handle the old man." He leaned forward, placing his now empty glass on the coffee table and moving Cherry's head from her lap. She didn't even stir.

"Take care of her. When the news breaks, she's going to need someone to relive all those horrors with. It's a lot."

I nodded, looking over the face of the sleeping girl on my couch.

"No one will ever hurt her again." It was a promise to them both.

Chapter Twenty-Four

Cherry

"How are you feeling today, Cherry?" Dr. Shelby asked, sitting across from me in the plush seats of her office.

"It's been…hard." I was still in a bit of shock after walking into my apartment last night to find Bunny. The ache of a hangover causing my temples to throb. Maybe I shouldn't have downed an entire bottle of whiskey last night.

"I can imagine with the things you've had to deal with over the past few hours. Coming home to that sort of scene and everything with your father's company this morning."

"That's an understatement." I took a sip of my hot coffee, enjoying the burn of the liquid.

The Vahn empire had fallen this morning. My father's assets seized, and he was under investigation for human trafficking, pedophilia, and an array of other charges. Not only was my father charged, but so were many of his business partners. Images and videos leaked online of the things they'd done with children. Some of those videos were of Zack and I. Just another thing to add to the list of why this damned city was a hellhole. Every man who'd ever touched me was now sitting in a cell. Never able to hurt me or anyone else. None of them having enough money to ever make this go away.

Dr. Shelby was still talking, but I'd stopped listening. Nodding and answering questions generically as needed. I didn't want to be here. I didn't want to talk to anyone about any of it. There was no desire in me to see the pity in their eyes.

Jackson was still out there and he'd had the nerve to have a stuffed animal dog with a dozen roses sent to my apartment this morning. It had caused a whole new wave of tears until I felt numb to everything.

Dimitri sat outside in the waiting area, afraid to leave me alone. Honestly, I couldn't blame him. He had taken care of everything last night, put out a search for

Jackson, and yet I still felt nothing. There was an ache in my chest that I couldn't deal with right now.

I just wanted to sleep.

To forget that all this had happened.

"I'd like to see you again next week to make sure you're doing alright. Here is my personal number. Please call if you need anything." Dr. Shelby handed me a card, her number scribbled in dark blue ink on the bottom.

"Thank you."

I sat the mug on the table before walking out of her office. Dimitri stood, buttoning his suit jacket one handed as he made his way over to me when I walked through the door.

Normally, that would have been attractive, but I just looked away. My life had never been perfect, but I'd finally felt like things were going good yesterday morning. Now my life was a hell I just wanted to escape.

Something in me was so broken that there was no way to put the pieces back together. I would just ruin everything I touched.

Just like always.

Chapter Twenty-Five

Cherry

It had been days, maybe even weeks, since I'd walked in to find Bunny massacred in my apartment. I couldn't get the image out of my head. The nightmares from before morphing with this new one until I couldn't sleep. If I wasn't taking sleeping pills and drinking enough that I couldn't walk, I'd just wake up screaming.

My life had turned into a never-ending nightmare that I couldn't escape.

There were monsters in every dark corner of my mind. Feeding off the anguish that seemed to consume me.

Dimitri, Zack and Damon tried to help, but nothing was working. The numbness and exhaustion taking over until I was barely functioning. Why Dimitri let me stay here and take care of me, I would never understand.

Apparently my father's trial was today, but I couldn't care less what they did to him at this point. He was a man who hid the evil of his business partners. He'd known about what they did to women and children. What they'd done to me and Zack during our younger years. He'd never cared so long as the deeds continued to fill his bank account. He may not have touched us himself, but he was just as sick as they were.

Dr. Shelby was now in contact with Dimitri. Speaking to him over the phone whenever he had questions. She thought it best to give me time. But he was worried.

On top of dealing with my less than human existence right now, he was also working with Damon to find Jackson. I couldn't leave the house and he was still sending shit to the door every morning. Dimitri finally said that anything addressed to me would be thrown out immediately. He was afraid to leave me alone, but he couldn't take care of me and find the man responsible for my newest breakdown..

I wish I was stronger. That I was better able to handle all the bullshit life kept throwing at me. I wasn't that type of person, though. I was weak and a plague on anyone who ever tried to care about me.

At this point, maybe it was all my fault. Maybe I was the problem. Maybe I was just unlovable.

Why would anyone want to deal with me?

I should just pack a bag and leave. Leave and never turn back. Start a new life on my own. Somewhere that no one would ever recognize me.

That's what I'd do. I'd just leave.

At the thought, I stood from the bed, careful not to wake Dimitri sleeping next to me. As quietly as I could, I started throwing things into my bag. This wouldn't be enough. With a new surge of energy I crept out of the apartment, moving to my own and slowly opening the door. Closing my eyes before flipping on the lights.

I was scared to see the blood again. The image of a knife sticking out of Bunny's side flashing behind my closed eyelids. I had to breathe through my nose, the lingering scent of bleach filling my nose.

Of course Dimitri had the place cleaned.

"Come on Cherry. You don't have time for this." I whispered to myself, fingers fisting at my sides as I slowly opened my eyes. Nothing looked any different.

Everything was in its place, every trace of Bunny erased from the space save for the washed pink food and water bowl that were left to dry on the counter.

Walking over I picked up one of the ceramic bowls. Running my fingers lightly over the rim before placing it back down.

Moving to my room I noticed that some things were missing or out of place. But overall it was clean. Going into the closet, I pulled out my carry-on suitcase and began throwing some essentials into it. Not caring if it was organized. Dimitri could wake up at any moment and I wanted to be out of here.

A quick look at my phone screen told me it was nearly one in the morning.

Just a few more minutes and I'd be out of here.

Lastly, I grabbed my wallet, passport, and car keys. Pulling my bags down the hall and into the elevator. Every second making anxiety filter through the numbness.

I didn't have time to second guess what I was doing. Throwing the bags into my car and peeling out of the parking lot as quickly as I could. Only making one stop at a small convenience store before heading to the airport.

After purchasing a one-way ticket to Mexico, I rushed into the bathroom, pulling out the box of hair dye I'd grabbed at the convenience store. It said it was golden-mahogany, but all I saw was brown. I needed to make sure no one noticed me. What better way than to have a plain brown hair color instead of my blonde hair?

I rushed a bit when applying the color, not letting it sit long enough to get too dark. But looking in the mirror I could barely recognize the girl staring back at me. This would do and I could do something different with it once I arrived at my destination.

Using the hand dryer mounted on the wall, I dried my hair so that it wasn't dripping wet. Next was to toss the phone. I was sure that Dimitri could track it with the help of Damon's tech guy. Pulling the battery out of it, I smashed it on the corner of the counter, shattering the screen, and tossed it into the trash along with the box of color.

Checking my ticket, I still had an hour to get through security and to my gate before the plane would leave.

My heart raced in my chest as I looked in that damn mirror again.

"It's for the best."

Grabbing my small bag and carry-on, I walked out of the bathroom. Shoulders back and head held high as I made my way to the security check. At this time of night, the place was fairly empty as I moved towards the chained off areas of TSA.

Before I could make it through the chained off aisles, a hand grabbed my wrist. Whipping around to look into the most beautiful ocean blue eyes I'd ever seen. The ones that starred in every wonderful dream I'd ever had.

"Dimitri," my words failed me as I looked into his disheveled face. He hadn't shaved, hair wasn't neatly combed or styled, a white t-shirt and sweatpants with his running shoes. He'd woken up and hadn't bothered to actually dress when he realized I was gone.

"Where do you think you were running off to, princess?" He pulled me closed, breath fanning over my lips.

"It's better for everyone if I leave." I whispered as his hand slid into my hair, pulling the now brown strands lightly through his thumb and forefinger. A look of regret flashing over his handsome face.

"You aren't going anywhere, Cherry. Even if I have to chain your ass to the bed to keep you. The moment you gave yourself to me you were mine. Forever." His lips found mine, soft yet demanding as he consumed me.

A small spark ignited in my heart that I hadn't felt since everything had gone to shit.

"You're mine, princess."

I wasn't sure if he was saying it to convince me or himself.

Chapter Twenty-Six

Dimitri

The glass crashed against the wall. The drink inside sliding down to the tiled floor as I panted in anger.

"Jensen is close. As soon as I get the location, he's all yours." Damon didn't even blink at my outburst. Taking a lazy drink from his own glass.

He and Jensen had been working all night and day looking for that bastard.

"He sent her a fucking stuffed dog the morning after, Damon. Like he was trying to rub it in her face that he'd gotten so close. It's solid proof that he's behind what she walked into last night. He just keeps sending shit. Every morning I get a call and have to tell security to throw it out. She already fucking left once."

My fingers racked through my hair. For once, I didn't care how unprofessional I looked. Now I did look more like my brother. The beginnings of a beard starting to grow where I hadn't bothered to shave. Not since dragging Cherry back home from the airport. Cherry was broken, and I had no clue how to make things better. Anything would be better than this hollow shell she'd become.

"How is she doing?" My brother asked, sounding bored, but I knew how much Cherry meant to him. She was like his little sister and he'd always looked out for her.

"I don't know." I sighed, sliding into the seat next to him. It had been four days since she'd tried to run off. I'd taken her passport and her money to make sure she had no way to go anywhere else. I wouldn't lose her, not even to herself.

Cherry hadn't been right since that night. Refusing to talk to me or anyone else. She'd barely spoken with her therapist either when Dr. Shelby called for emergency appointments. She wouldn't even look at me. Not since I'd found her at the airport. She just sat around and staring into space. I didn't know how to help her with any of it. Too much had happened in so short a time.

"Zack said that he couldn't get her to talk, either. It'll take her some time. That girl's been through one hell of a life. Worse than we ever had it." Damon moved to pour us both fresh glasses from the crystal decanter that was now the centerpiece of my office desk.

I had no business being here, but after Zack had outed his father and business partners, my father had been calling everyone in. Making sure that he and the company couldn't be tied to any of the Vahn dealings. I wasn't in the headspace to deal with it. Everything screaming at me to actually chain Cherry to the damn bed every time I had to leave, but a few well-placed cameras allowed me to watch her while I had to be away. Every muscle strained to hurt the man responsible for Cherry's life going up in flames.

We'd taken down her father. He'd be dead in less than a week thanks to a few informants. A little money passing hands, and a couple of phone calls now that his trial had sentenced him to life. No one liked someone who hurt children, especially in prison.

Now there was just Jackson Stewart.

"Maybe try fucking it out of her." My dumbass brother joked, taking another swig from his glass.

He had an interesting way of looking at things, but maybe he had a point. Something had to get through to her didn't it? That kiss at the airport had almost gotten through to her. A spark lighting in those jade green eyes for only a second before fading.

Damon's phone rang, and he picked up before the first ring even finished. A wide, sadistic smile spread over his face. With the long hair and beard, he looked like a viking ready for war with that look on his face.

I sat forward, taking a drink from the glass in my hand as he finished the phone conversation. He downed his drink, setting the glass on the desk as he stood to leave.

"Gott 'em." The smile never left his face as he walked out.

Tonight, that fucker would die by my hands.

Chapter Twenty-Seven

Cherry

The click of the door woke me from my restless sleep. I'd been sleeping on this couch all day and hadn't bothered to move after Dimitri had left after getting a work call.

I didn't want to eat. I just wanted to sleep.

"Princess," Dimitri knelt on the floor in front of me, his fingers slipping into my still brown hair. "I need you to get up. I have something to show you."

"I can't leave. He's out there." My voice coming out sounding tired and scratchy from lack of use.

"I promised, I will keep you safe…"

I didn't give him a chance to finish his sentence, sitting up and pushing him back by the shoulders. "No."

Anger flashed in those ocean eyes as we both stood, him towering over me, doing nothing to deter the glare I sent in his direction.

"Is that how it's going to be princess?" His words were filled with a venom I'd never heard directed at me. A thrill rushing up my spine as fear and anger fought back the numbness.

I should be scared of him. I knew he wasn't a good guy. He'd probably killed people for far less, but I didn't care. Shoving him back again.

A growl left his chest as he reached for me. In the quickest of movements, he had my arms behind my back and my front pressed into the couch. A screech of rage left me as I fought to pull my arms free from his vice-like grip. The numbness gave way to a rage I'd never felt before as Dimitri pressed himself atop my back, holding me in place as I fought for freedom.

"That's it, princess. Get angry. Take it all out on me if you must. I can take it. Give me every ounce of pain and rage in the pretty little body of yours." He growled in my ear before he let me go, getting off me to stand on the other side of the room.

As soon as I was free, I pushed from the cushions, grabbed the empty mug on the coffee table from this morning's tea and hurled it at his pretty fucking head.

A dark chuckle leaving him as the cup shattered against the wall behind him. "You'll have to do better than that."

Red blurred my vision and a scream of rage left me as I reached for anything within reach, throwing it at Dimitri. He simply moved out of the way of everything. Debris littered the floor of the living room until he was making his way towards me. His hand gripping the coffee table and flipping it out of the way as he inched closer again.

I'd run out of things to throw as he cornered me. My back pressed up against the wall. His hand wrapped around my throat to hold me in place as I bared my teeth at him.

"Are you finished?" He bared his teeth right back. Anger darkening his blue eyes.

I spit in his face, a grin twisting my lips as he used his free hand to wipe at his face. Making a tsking noise like he was dealing with a petulant child before his lips crashed to mine. The force bruising as he lifted me into his arms. My legs wrapped around his waist on instinct as he pressed me against the wall.

This wasn't like every other time. This time it was hateful, violent, and all-consuming as we bit and scratched at each other. He didn't bother undressing me as he pressed himself harder against me. Pinning me with his massive frame to the wall as he undid his pants, moving my panties to the side and slamming home.

All I could do was hold on as he fucked me into the drywall. It was fast and quick. Climaxing within a handful of thrusts, his name falling from my lips like a prayer as he fucked me through the pleasure. Growls and grunts left him as he bit and sucked on any exposed skin he could find. Biting my nipples through the thin fabric of my shirt until I was whimpering at the tenderness. Nails digging into his shoulders as I held onto him.

He was everywhere. The only thing I could focus on as he conquered me. Body and soul until we were both spent. His come filling me until it was dripping down my legs when he finally sat me on my feet. Moving my panties back into place.

The kisses and touches turned gentle as we came down from whatever the hell that had been.

"Get some pants on and don't you fucking dare clean up." He gripped me through my now soaked panties. Rubbing my clit through the material until I was moaning at his possessiveness, at his touches that set my blood on fire.

When he pulled away from me, stepping back enough to make room for me to move around him, my head felt clearer. The room, however, was completely trashed.

My cheeks heated at the realization that I'd done that. The whole thing was a blur, and I was having a hard time remembering exactly what happened. All I knew was that I'd felt numb, then angry, and now a calm had washed over me. My heart still ached, but for the first time in a long while I felt more like myself again.

Like surfacing after too much time underwater.

"Don't worry about it." Dimitri said, his fingers gripping my chin to force me to lock eyes with him. "It's fine, princess. Now get dressed. I'll clean up this mess and make a call for a cleaner."

"I'm sorry." My voice was weak, but he placed a soft kiss to my lips, not really a kiss at all.

"Dressed." His deep voice rumbling on the order, causing a shiver to run down my spine.

"Yes, sir."

Chapter Twenty-Eight

Cherry

When Dimitri had told me to get dressed, I hadn't been expecting to come to Hellfire, especially considering that it was closed right now.

With everything going on, Damon had closed the place for the next week until things could blow over. Right now, too much was in the air and we were all trying to stay out of the spotlight.

Entering through the back door in the alley, Dimitri took my hand and led me inside. A man screaming rang in my ears as we entered the club, shutting the back door quickly.

"Damon have a new plaything in the basement?" I asked, only half joking as Dimitri pulled me to the basement door and down the dark steps. The screams grew louder as we made it deeper into the darkness.

My hand tightened in Dimitri's hand as he opened the door to Damon's *playroom*. Bright lights flooding the dark areas of the basement.

An audible gasp leaving me at the sight before me.

Jackson was chained up, hanging from chains attached to the ceiling. One of his eye swollen shut and blood covered his once handsome features. His shirt hanging in tatters over his shoulder and a very obvious wet spot darkening the front of his jeans. A small puddle of blood accumulating underneath him on the plastic covered floor.

"Cherry. Cherry, please make him stop. He's fucking crazy. I didn't mean any of it. Please. I'm so sorry, baby. We can fix this." Jackson's words were filled with panic and gargled. IT looked like Damon had been pulling his teeth.

"I may have gotten ahead of myself," Damon scratched the back of his head, a childlike grin on his face as he turned to face us.

Dimitri's hand slid up my arm, bringing my focus back to him. "He will never hurt you again, princess. I just needed you to see that."

He handed me the keys to his car. "You can go see your brother. I'll be here awhile and don't want you to feel alone."

Brushing a kiss to my forehead he walked further into the room, tossing his jacket into a far corner. Fingers working to roll up his sleeves to expose muscular forearms. The veins were visible from here as he picked up one of the knives laid out for them.

"Dimitri." I couldn't take my eyes off him as he turned to face me, ocean eyes flaring bright. They were the hard eyes of a man about to get a payment in blood. "Make him hurt."

My words brought a smirk to his handsome face as I took a step out of the room.

"Anything for you, princess."

Chapter Twenty-Nine

Dimitri

The door closed with a loud click. Jackson's pleas grew louder as I eyed the knife in my hands.

"What took you so long, brother?" Damon asked, whipping his hands on a towel.

"Had something to take care of. Let's finish this."

We took our time, slowly skinning this piece of shit alive. Blood covered us and the floor as he screamed. Pain filled his voice as we sliced him over and over again. The sounds he made were a balm to my once dead heart, causing it to ache in a way I hadn't felt since childhood.

It ached for every tear I'd whipped from my goddess's face. For every time he'd broken her and abandoned her. For every time I was sure he fucked her before she was mine.

This fucker wasn't worth the time she'd given him. I'd spend the rest of my life righting every wrong ever done to her.

No one would ever hurt her again or they'd end up just like Jackson Stewart.

Just another missing person the world would move on without.

Chapter Thirty

Cherry

2 Months Later

Life had slowly gotten back to normal after everything with Jackson and my father. My father and many of his partners had been killed in a prison riot less than a week into his sentencing. I was sure that Dimitri had something to do with all of it, seeing as he hadn't seemed surprised by the news.

Father's assets were left to Zack who quickly liquidated the company, splitting everything with me. He wasn't willing to deal with any of it or let some idiot run the business. He was content working at Hellfire, and I honestly couldn't blame him. The Vahn Legacy would die with us.

As for Jackson, he was nowhere to be found. A missing person's report showing up about two weeks after his disappearance. The university offered candlelight visuals for their missing professor.

No one really knew what had happened other than Damon and Dimitri. I wasn't interested in knowing the details of what happened downstairs in that basement, either. I just knew that he'd never show up in my life again.

The unofficial story was that after being charged with having a relationship with a student he'd gotten depressed and gone AWOL. Thankfully, Dimitri had kept my name from being mentioned where that was concerned.

I'd officially moved in with Dimitri, making the apartment ours and getting back to our everyday life. It still felt weird not having Bunny around, but I couldn't imagine ever replacing her. Dimitri had charged Damon with getting her cremated, and now her urn sat on the top of our fireplace mantle.

He'd joked, very badly, about turning my old apartment into my own personal rage room after the incident of me throwing thing at his head. I hadn't found the idea entertaining in the slightest, instead insisting on upping my therapy appointments to twice a week. Dr. Shelby had even prescribed medication to help with the PTSD and depression. But I was getting better. Taking things one day at a time.

I spent most nights working at Hellfire while Dimitri took to working at home more often so that we could spend time together. He only went into the office once a week for late meetings while I was working my shifts.

On the days I wasn't working at Hellfire, I'd begun working as a counselor for underprivileged youth at the local center. Putting my schooling to good use while finishing my degree online. Nothing that happened would make me give up on the desire to help others. I couldn't hunt the bad guys like Damon did, or use a company board to right the wrongs of our fathers, but this I could do.

Tonight I was working a shorter shift at Hellfire, so I sent a text to Dimitri that I would grab dinner on the way to his office. He wanted me to meet him there tonight, saying that he had extra work he needed to finish before we headed home.

After everything, he still didn't want me to be left alone. Afraid that I might run away again. Nothing I said ever really convinced him otherwise. The brown mixed in with the natural blonde that was growing back a constant reminder of what I'd tried to do.

Checking my phone, I sent a quick text to let him know I'd be heading over in the next hour. A smile spread across my lips at his instant reply, saying that he missed me.

"Hey now, no sexting at work!" Zack yelled out, sliding a drink to me down the bar.

"Oh, shut up!" I yelled back, still smiling, as I added the drink to my tray for another round of deliveries.

My shift was finally over and I rushed out front to where a car was waiting to take me to Dimitri's office. It was a fairly short ride, and I was giddy at the prospect of a dinner date at his job. I'd never seen the office and I was excited to see the extravagance I was sure awaited me there.

After making a quick stop to grab my favorite tacos, we pulled up along an enormous skyscraper. The driver opened my door and escorted me inside to the elevator. Thanks to signs I was directed on how to get to Dimitri's office.

I looked so out of place here in my ripped denim skirt and faded band tee. I never would have managed to live up to this elegant lifestyle 24/7. How Dimitri did it I would never understand.

The elevator chimed as I made my way to the fortieth floor and took the route the downstairs signs had told me to go. The entire place was dark, save for a few lights here and there. Finding the corner office was fairly easy as I knocked on the fogged glass door that read *Executive Vice President Ashfood* on a golden plaque. The handles of the door shone gold in the low lighting, too.

"Come in." Came the muffled voice of my lover. A smile spread across my face as I pushed through the door into his darkly lit office.

An insane view lit up the floor to ceiling windows. Showcasing the beauty of the city. His modern desk was placed strategically in the center. Rows of built-in shelves lined the walls full of awards, antiques, and leather-bound books. With the type of book snob Dimitri was, I was sure that most, if not all, would be first editions of all the classics and his favorites..

The view only made more mesmerizing by the god of a man standing there, back to me as he looked out the window, as if watching his lessors on the streets below. My body grew hot at the power and confidence that rolled off him in waves. He had discarded his suit jacket at some point, now only dressed in his slacks and a white button-down shirt. The sleeves rolled up to showcase the arms I loved so much.

"Undress and crawl to me." He ordered without turning to face me as the door shut behind me. Leaving me feeling completely trapped.

With only a moment's hesitation, I sat the bag of food down and began to undress. Tossing my skirt, t-shirt, and thong into a pile near the door. Descending to my knees as I slowly crawled towards him and that massive window.

He only turned to face me once I was directly behind him, still kneeling on the floor. His ocean eyes shining brightly in the dim lights as his fingertips brushed my cheek tenderly.

"My princess. My goddess. So fucking perfect." He praised, sliding his thumb over my lips. "Now undo my pants and take me in that sweet mouth."

My fingers shook slightly as I reached up to undo his belt and pants. Not wanted to fuck this up. He didn't always order me around like this, but when he did, I craved every second. Wanting to give him all of me. To worship him like my own personal deity.

With little effort, I freed his throbbing erection, wrapping my hand around its base to work him slowly with my hand.

"In your mouth, princess." He hissed in pleasure as I stroked his length. His hand moving to slip into my hair as if forcing himself not to take complete control.

I smiled up at him through my lashes. Moving my hand slowly along his length and only taking the tip between my lips. Making this slow and tortuous for him.

The grip on my hair tightened as the veins of his arms protruded, showing just how much he was holding back as I continued to tease him with my mouth.

Without warning, he smacked my hand away, plunging his cock into my throat. A gag caused my throat to tighten around him as I attempted to breathe between each of his thrusts. Both of his hands tangling in my hair as he fucked my mouth. Tears streamed down my face as my nails dug into his muscular thighs.

Chapter Thirty-One

Cherry

I had zero control here.

I was at his mercy.

My pussy clenching on nothing and my sex dripping down my thighs as I took him deep into my throat. The hands in my hair fisted and pulling on the roots, the pain mixing with pleasure as Dimitri used me for his own pleasure.

In my wildest dreams, I'd fantasized about this happening, but the reality was so much better than I ever could have imagined. Him in this place, with me, of all people. Using me for his own pleasure and still willing to stop should I ever ask him to.

Never in a million years had I ever thought that he would choose to be with me.

I'd never been so turned on in my life and he hadn't even touched me yet. The ache in my core became unbearable every time he thrust into my mouth. Wishing it was being filled instead.

Glancing up through my lashes, I took in his less than pristine dress shirt. Him being fully dressed and me naked at his feet should have been demeaning, but I'd never seen this man so disheveled. He was so put together all the time. Even when preparing to take a man's life for me, he'd been an image of male perfection.

At my hands, he was less put together. His mask breaking with every thrust of his cock down my throat. His blue eyes were such a dark blue they looked black from his hunger. The sounds of pleasure left him in a deep rumble as I worked his length in and out of my mouth. Taking him as deep as I could. All of it was for me. Because of me. And I'd never felt so powerful. So loved and cared for.

"Fuck, Cherry." He groaned out, head falling back against the window in pleasure as I cupped his balls and swallowed around his length.

Again, my pussy clenched. I could come from this alone and I still wanted more. I wanted all of him. To worship this man who made me feel loved and cherished. Who didn't see me as a broken little doll.

I felt his balls draw up in my hand before I was yanked forcefully off his throbbing dick. A whimper leaving me at the loss of contact and the force he had on my hair.

He pulled me up, walking us over to his desk chair where he pulled me into his lap. Forcing me to straddle him in the chair that was definitely not built for two people. His arm wrapped around my waist to hold me steady as his lips crashed against mine.

I could feel his length rubbing against my wet folds. But with his grip around me I couldn't force him inside.

A low growl left his chest as he thrust his hips against me. Rubbing himself through my slick. The mushroom head hit against my clit until I was shuddering with need.

So close and yet so far from the release my body craved.

"So fucking wet for me." His voice came out raspy, filled with a need for me that burned. Burned like the sweetest of fires I'd ever known. I wanted to die in its blaze. If only he would allow me.

"You're so responsive. Do you want my cock inside this tight pussy?"

I moaned out a yes. Lost to the feeling of him rubbing against me. The wet sounds filled the air, and my fingers dug into his dress shirt, fisting the fabric so hard I was surprised my nails didn't rip through the material.

"Please, sir." I begged, tears burning the backs of my eyes as he held me firm against him.

His lips grazed mine softly. "Use your words, princess."

"Dimitri, I need you inside me."

God, I needed him more than I needed air.

"Inside you where?" His lips trailed down my neck and chest. Taking a budded nipple between his teeth before sucking it into his warm mouth. His tongue flicked against the sensitive flesh.

"I need you in my pussy. Please, Dimitri, I can't stand it."

"Good girl." He praised, shifting his hips and sheathing his cock into my weeping cunt with a single thrust.

Groans of pleasure left us at the same moment as he seated himself deep. He was so big. Bigger than I'd ever had and a sharp pain mingled with the pleasure like it always did when he slipped inside.

Everything came together in an explosion behind my eyes as he began to thrust up into me. His hands found my waist to grind me on his length, creating the perfect friction against my g-spot and clit.

"I'm going to fuck this tight pussy, then I'm going to fill you up here."

I felt the press of his finger against my back hole. Teasing the ring of muscle without pressing inside or his thrusts faltering.

"Yes," I moaned. not caring how needy and broken I sounded at this moment.

"Has anyone ever fucked this tight little hole, princess?"

His finger slipped to my pussy, sliding back to my ass, leaving a slick trail. Giving no warning as he pushed a long digit inside at the same time he thrust into me.

A scream of pleasure left me as my walls convulsed around his hard shaft. I'd never come so hard in my life and he fucked me through it all. His cock and finger worked in sync to draw out my pleasure as I came and came.

"That's it. Get me nice and wet so I can fuck that sexy ass."

He stood from his chair, and I wrapped myself around him to keep from falling. Arm swiping out to clear off his desk before he lay me atop the cold, wooden surface. Not once did his cock leave my dripping heat.

Prying my hands from his shirt he pinned them above my head in one of his large hands. My legs braced on his shoulders as he towered over me with such dominance I couldn't help the moan of pleasure that left me.

He thrust into me one last time before pulling out, moving his other hand to position the tip of his cock at my back entrance.

"Take a deep breath for me, princess. And try to relax." His words were a soft command as he dragged his tip from my ass to my clit and back again.

On the second pass, he told me to breathe, and I did as he'd instructed. Gasping hard as he pushed into my tight hole. Inch by inch, he pushed into me. Giving just a small fraction of time between each muscle he stretched past.

"Relax," he cooed, hand moving to my clit as he pushed in deeper. A whimper left me as he worked my clit with his expert fingers. Every second caused my muscles to relax further as he pushed into me.

I was so wet and aroused that he slid in with little resistance until he was seated fully in my ass. Holding his hips still and fucking me with his fingers until I was pliant in his hands.

He praised me, leaning down to capture my lips as he slowly began to move. Groaning against my mouth as my body clenched around his cock and fingers.

"Such a good girl, princess." He breathed, beginning to move his hips and fingers at a leisurely pace. Filling me up in the best sort of pain and pleasure I'd ever felt.

My head swam as I was pushed closer and closer to the edge of my undoing. I wasn't even aware that sex could be this consuming. A fire that burned through my veins until I was delirious with need.

"Oh, fuck. Dimitri, I'm going to…" I moaned as he pushed his hips faster. The wet sounds of skin hitting skin filling the room only heightened the heat that coiled in my belly. Like a serpent waiting to strike.

"Come for me princess." He growled, slamming into me until I wasn't sure where I ended and he began.

At the command, I came with a scream, my back arching off the desk and my hands strained in his iron grip above my head. His cock continued to slide in and out of me quickly as my ass clenched around the length of him. My pussy soaking his hand and a pool of my cream puddling underneath me.

I thought it would be over quickly, but his skilled fingers and dick held me in pleasure's grip. The sounds I made were animalistic as I came again and again.

"I can't. I can't." Tears spilled down my face as I moaned, forced to keep coming until I lost sense of everything I was.

"You can," he growled, thrusting his hips faster, his hands moving to my hips to lift me further from the desk, changing where he hit inside me as he fucked me mercilessly.

I needed something to hold on to as the pressure in my belly began to build again. Gasping for breath, I gripped the edge of the desk above my now free hands, throwing my head back in complete ecstasy.

I was going to come just from him fucking my ass. It was dirty and depraved, and I wanted more. This man would be my ruin and I didn't care so long as he kept worshiping me like this.

"Give me one more." His cock throbbed in my ass, pelvis working against my clit creating delicious friction.

"Dimitri," I moaned out as he bottomed out and another orgasm was ripped from me.

He followed right after me, fingers digging into my hips until I was sure I'd bruise. A groan of my name on his lips as I felt him fill up my ass.

My vision was blurring at the edges as he pulled from me. Leaving me completely boneless on his desk.

I was so out of it that I hadn't noticed him going to the bathroom that connected to his office. He'd come back dressed in a fresh pair of dress pants slung low on his hips and a clean dress shirt left open. Showcasing the toned muscles he worked hard to maintain. That delicious v that had me nearly drooling.

He pulled my legs open, spreading me out on the desk once more. It was then I noticed the wet rag in his hand. I could only lay there, trying to catch my breath, as he made quick work of cleaning me up. When he was finished, he pulled me into his lap in his desk chair and wrapped a white dress shirt around my shoulders.

I was so…happy and safe. My eyes drifted closed no matter how many times I tried to blink them open.

I felt his lips press against my temple as he held me close to his chest and I relaxed into his embrace.

"Dimitri," I whispered, my eyes feeling heavier as I buried my face in his neck. Letting the scent of him - spice, amber and oak - overwhelm my senses.

"Rest, princess. I will wake you to eat something in a moment," was the last thing I heard before my world turned black.

Chapter Thirty-Two

Cherry

I awoke to the sun streaming through the large open windows of Dimitri's bedroom. Every muscle aching in protest as I pulled the covers over my head, something catching the light as I opened my eyes underneath the blankets.

There was just enough light filtering through the fabric that I could see what caught my eye. On the ring finger of my left hand, there was now a ring that hadn't been there before. The same rose gold ring I'd looked at during the auction.

I sat up in bed, tossing the covers as I frantically searched for Dimitri.

"Dimitri?" I asked, walking out into the kitchen and living area of the penthouse. The doors to the outdoor patio left open to let in a warm breeze.

I took a step closer, pushing the billowing curtains out of the way as I made my way outside. The entire deck was set up with a trail of pink rose petals leading towards a sitting area. The entire thing was set up with an array of breakfast pastries and fruit. An ice bucket with sparkling wine chilling within and flutes of what appeared to be mimosas. The table was set for two as Dimitri stood next to it in a pair of navy blue dress pants and a white button up, the top 2 buttons left undone and the sleeves rolled up.

"What is all this?" I asked as he walked over, taking my hand in his to pull me towards the table where breakfast was set up.

"Cherry," he said, dropping to a knee before me. "These past few months have been the best and worst time of our lives. The day I woke up to find you gone, I knew I'd never be able to live without you. Life has no meaning without you. I know being with me won't make your life any easier, but I will do everything in my power to make sure you are safe and cared for. Princess," his finger traced over the pink diamond on the band now gracing my finger.

"Will you marry me?"

Chapter Thirty-Three

Cherry

1 Year Later

The music was loud, the place packed, and drinks were flowing as Zack and I worked our asses off to serve all the paying customers of Hellfire.

"We really need someone else to help on nights like this," I yelled to Zack as I handed off a beer to one guy at the bar.

"Well, if I find someone, I'll hire them on the spot." Zack smiled his crooked grin, telling me how serious he was taking the idea.

I rolled my eyes, thanking the next patron before loading up a tray to take upstairs to the VIP room where Damon and Dimitri were meeting their father tonight.

"I'll be right back. Gonna go drop these off upstairs and then head back to help with the bar.

"Alright. Damon is on his way to check on the door, then will be up later. Don't get too distracted with that husband of yours, Mrs. Ashford." Zack threw a wink in my direction.

Ever since we eloped a few months ago, Zack has given me shit that he wasn't invited to a wedding. There hadn't been a wedding at all. Just a simple courthouse thing with no one in attendance.

No one even knew we were married. Dimitri thought it would be safer to keep it secret while he and Damon worked on a plan to dethrone their father. That man had some business partners who wouldn't hesitate to use loved ones as payback.

Slipping upstairs, I delivered the drinks to the men in suits, making sure to keep my distance as Dimitri stood off to the side talking with his father. I could feel his eyes on me as I left the room, not looking in his direction as I left. My finger reaching up to finger the ring on a chain around my neck. The same rose gold ring he had proposed with what felt like so long ago.

Not even his father knew we were married, or even seeing each other. The only people who knew the truth were the two people closest to us.

As I made my way back downstairs, I slipped off to grab some orders from the other areas of the club. Noticing Damon with a raven haired beauty at the bar getting drinks. She was dressed to kill. Showing off all the art covering her skin, and blood-red lips painted to perfection.

They were leaving as I rounded the bar, elbowing Zack to get his attention.

"Who was that?" I asked, nodding towards the retreating pair.

"Her name is Angel I guess. Just some chick that caught the boss's attention." His grin was almost wicked as he looked after the two of them walking off in the crowd. "She's going to eat him alive."

"Like you have room to talk. I can't wait to see the girl who snags you up. Whoever she is, she's going to walk all over you." I joked half-heartedly, getting back to work on making drinks for all the paying customers.

Tonight was going to be one hell of a night for Hellfire.

187

Also by Hayley Briana

The Hellfire Series

Angel of Blood

Angel in Chains

Sweetest of Fires

Hellfire

Fires of Damnation (coming 2024)

Darkside Fairytales

Belong to Me

All Mad (coming 2024)

Be My Guest (coming soon)

On the Hook (coming soon)

Haunting Series

My Dark Haunting

My Dark Terror

My Dark Dolly

My Dark Ending

Haunting

Fall Series

Fall From Grace (coming 2024)

Fall to Sin (coming soon)

Love Me Series

Love Me in the Dark

Love Me in the Moonlight (coming soon)

About the Author

Hayley Briana is an indie author currently residing in Colorado. As a mom & wife, she finds herself in need of some major self-care in the form of a good cup of coffee (or wine) and a good book. Escaping into a world of fantasy is Hayley's favorite pass time outside her day-to-day responsibilities. When she's not adulting or writing, you can most likely find her tucked away in her home library.

For more info on Hayley and what she is working on please visit HayleyBrianaWrites.com

Follow Hayley on Social

Instagram.com/hbrianawrites

TikTok.com/@beautyandthebookcase

www.ingramcontent.com/pod-product-compliance
Lightning Source LLC
Chambersburg PA
CBHW040822010826
48978CB00012BB/582